W9-BCL-996

TRANSPORT
7-4I-R

TRANSPORT 7-41-R

T. DEGENS

The Viking Press   New York

FIRST EDITION

Copyright © 1974 by T. Degens
All rights reserved
First published in 1974 by The Viking Press, Inc.
625 Madison Avenue, New York, N.Y. 10022
Published simultaneously in Canada by
The Macmillan Company of Canada Limited
Printed in U.S.A.

1   2   3   4   5   78   77   76   75   74

Library of Congress Cataloging in Publication Data
Degens, T.   Transport 7–41–R.
Summary: A thirteen-year-old girl describes her journey
from the Russian sector of defeated Germany to Cologne
on a transport carrying returning refugees in 1946.
[1. Germany—History—Allied occupation, 1945—Fiction.
2. World War, 1939–1945—Refugees—Fiction]   I. Title.
PZ7.D3637Tr   [Fic]   74–10930

ISBN 0–670–72429–7

TRANSPORT
7-41-R

I

TRANSPORT 7-41-R
REPATRIATION OF EVACUEES TO COLOGNE
Departure: April 25, 1946, 8:25 A.M.
PERSONS WITHOUT AUTHORIZATION ARE STRICTLY
FORBIDDEN TO BOARD THE TRAIN.

I DID NOT DARE TO
leave my place and I did not speak with anyone. For
seven hours I sat in the open doorway of the boxcar
and waited. Time enough to read the announcement
again and again. I read it forward and I read it backward; I counted the letters and rearranged the numbers and felt comforted when they added up to 54. A
lucky number—my birthday! I had turned thirteen on
the fifth of April of this year.

Around me people wandered in and out of the cars
and filled the platform. We were supposed to be
evacuees from Cologne—people who during the war
had been sent out of the industrial and therefore more
heavily bombed part of Germany into the countryside. Now, one year after the German defeat, the

9

Russians, the French, the British, and the Americans, who had split the country in four parts, each occupying one zone, were allowing the evacuees to return.

I wondered how many of us were really evacuees or had ever lived in or near Cologne. I tried to think why the others wanted to leave the Russian zone and where they got their false papers and if they had bribed their local officials with butter and eggs as mother had. One pound of butter and two dozen eggs. How cheap to get rid of me.

At 3:17 in the afternoon the transport finally left. There was no warning. A sudden violent jolt tore through the railroad cars, and they screeched and rattled. That alerted the crowds on the platform. Furious, the people searched for someone responsible —someone in uniform—to make the train stop. I saw arms raised in protest and there were angry shouts.

"Where the hell is the stationmaster?"

"Get the engineer off the engine!"

"Stop the train! For heaven's sake, stop the train!"

I saw three women charge up to an armed guard, then break away abruptly and meekly withdraw into the crowd. They had charged up to the wrong uniform: the man was a Russian soldier and not a German railroad clerk. They could have caused a lot of trouble—certainly a renewed delay. The whole transport could have been ordered home and they could have landed in prison. How could people still make such a mistake after one year of occupation? The uniforms were not even similar.

The train was inching along. With a wail the crowd broke apart and scrambled for the open doors. I was pushed aside from my watchpost and trampled and kicked and blinded. An enormous bosom pressed into my face and pinned me against the wall. I wiggled and stretched to keep from suffocating. How had she managed to stay so fat? Almost all the people I knew were thin and hungry. A farmer's wife, perhaps a black market expert with her suitcase full of bread, jam, butter, and sausages. I wanted to stay close, yet I needed air, so I nudged her and she noticed my plight and shifted her weight. I squeezed to my former place and looked out.

The battle was over. People had reboarded the train and now leaned out of doors and waved and shouted. The train trundled slowly along the platform, and scores of waving, weeping, crying, and shouting relatives and friends accompanied it.

"Write, you hear! Write as often as you can! Don't forget us!"

"Tell Aunt Gerda about Horst! He needs that medicine!"

"There's still two hundred grams of sugar on my ration card! In the top drawer of the desk!"

"Good-by, good-by! We'll see you!"

I longed for someone I knew, one of my family, any familiar face. Someone to wave to and cry with and share the bitterness of parting so I would not feel so terribly lonely. But they were all strangers and their faces blurred through my tears.

I pulled my handkerchief out and waved at everybody and everything indiscriminately: the men and women and children, the Russian guards, the station, the city. We were rolling faster now, bumping over

II

crossings, nosing into the right track. With a shock I realized that the train was heading westward, along the same route that I had come early in the morning on my way to the district capital, where such transports as ours assembled. We would have to pass through my home town and I did not want to see it again so soon. I had taken leave this morning. I had looked hard at my house, my street; I had walked with my head turned back to the small station. I had etched every line into my brain till it hurt.

I did not want to see it again so soon.

Yet I looked out. First the outskirts of the district capital, bare ruins of burned-out houses. In a couple of weeks they would disappear under green, but spring was late and this winter had been colder than anything people could remember, or did it only seem that way with the shortage of coal and the electricity shut off for hours? The April sun was just beginning to warm a little. Now the soccer field, the deer park, subdivided since the first year of the war into tiny garden plots. What had happened to the deer?

Then fields and woods, a village with its fat farmhouses hidden under trees. More fields, brown and overgrown with weeds instead of shining green with winter wheat. The farmers had baked the seed corn into bread during the winter.

For a moment the spire of our church, then woods again, tall silver-gray stems of beeches.

Another village.

Over there the estate, where they made us pick potatoes in the fall of '44 to help the war effort. My whole grade, some thirty kids, had been ordered into that field. It was cold, wet, miserable, the end of October. And we were not really strong enough for the work. They had machines running around the field that coughed up potatoes, spewed them out incessantly, and we, our feet swollen to gigantic size with lumps of wet earth, huddled on the ground and picked them up and filled large, heavy baskets and emptied them into burlap bags. No matter how we scrambled, we had never cleared the ground before the machine sputtered along and covered it again. Soon we had fallen hopelessly behind and only Lisa's fainting saved us—gave us time to catch up. She fainted right into the machine's path and they had to stop. What a talent she had!

Nobody had touched the field since.

Another village. The fieldworkers' cottages. The church, older and smaller than the one in my town. The monks had built their first settlement here, when they came nine hundred years ago from the west.

Before the war was lost, they had taught us in school that the land had been uninhabited before the arrival of the monks and that they had cleared the woods and drained the swamps and brought in people from the west. Last year, after the Allied victory, the same teachers taught us that there had been people there all along—Sorbs and Wends and Slavs—and that the monks had taken their land and converted them by force or killed them and driven the lucky ones into hiding. The same teachers taught it with a straight face.

First you got an A for no Sorbs.

Then you got an A for Sorbs.

It does not really matter to me if my ancestors—father's people (mother's came with the railroads a hundred years ago)—were Sorbs, Wends, or Slavs or immigrants from the west. Why can't we forget whose side they were on?

I know nothing about my great-great-grandparents. I know nothing about my great-grandparents. I know hardly anything about my grandparents, though I do know that Grandfather drowned while ice-skating on the duck pond the year I was born and that some people called it an accident. Others hinted that his death had something to do with the closing of our local bank. There was no way of telling who was right. Grandfather had worked at the bank all his life. Grandmother fell sick and died a month later.

So why should I care about such distant relatives and get angry now about what happened to them? Yet when the same people teach you first one thing and then another, without even winking at you to show that they are only following orders, that makes me angry.

A manor house, once out of sight and mysteriously beautiful behind century-old chestnuts and oaks, was now exposed to view. People had cut the trees for firewood. It looked small, naked, shabby, deflated, the windows covered with cardboard and plywood, the walls smudged with smoke. The owners had fled and refugees from the eastern provinces had crowded into every square foot of space. Even if they had wanted to do something about its decay, there were no tools, no material.

Beech woods on the left, a long row of identical

small houses on the right. The train slowed as we approached the station of my home town. The platform was empty. Nobody expected us and we rolled through without stopping. The buildings still wore their protective coloring against planes and bombs. Countless graffiti were scratched into the ugly dirt brown. I had written one too. Nothing to be proud of. A simple message to my brother Wolfgang, telling him how stupid he was. The train picked up speed.

We passed through a tunnel of tall, silver-gray beeches, and the town lay hidden behind them. How I loved those woods. Here we had cut our very own tree last winter (instead of coal the town allotted live trees for fuel). "Timber!" we cried when the beech trembled and groaned and then crashed toward us, and we leaped away at the very last moment. Here I collected mushrooms. Here I had picked the spring's first anemones, the yellow cowslip, woodruff for the linen cupboard. Here we got our feet wet more than a hundred times in the zigzagging creek. Here I spent hours on my knees gathering beech kernels that could be exchanged for small amounts of cooking oil. The blueberry bushes seldom bore fruit, yet each year I checked them.

A clearing opened onto the stadium, where I had marched in different uniforms: first in the dark-blue skirt, white blouse, and brown jacket of the Hitler Youth, then as a Young Pioneer with a bright blue neckerchief. We had sung different songs and had carried different flags and those who yelled the orders had changed with the uniforms.

For another short moment the spire of our church.

The last glimpse—for how long? I did not know. I felt a lump in my throat. Did I really want to leave? But there was no time to think about it now. I had to look for my bag, find a better place for myself.

I soon discovered how stupid I had been in taking my long farewell. Everyone else had secured his territory, marked its boundaries with bundles, suitcases, boxes, and bedrolls, and was watching over it. When I turned around I was met with ugly stares that seemed to say: *"Stay where you are!"* *"No room for you here!"* *"Don't dare come closer."* They had been ugly ever since I had arrived this morning . . .

2

FIRST SOME OPINION-ated clerks in the barracks outside the half-wrecked railroad station of the district capital had refused me my final papers, though I had been assigned to this transport for weeks. I had traveled alone from my town. Mother and father did not dare take a day off from work and they never considered Wolfgang a substitute companion.

"Kids can't go alone," they had said at the barracks. "This is a special transport for families evacuated during the war who must return to their former homes in Cologne!"

"But I *am* returning to my former home in Cologne!" I insisted. It was not true, but I carried papers to prove it. Not too expensive papers and therefore perhaps not too convincing. You could get papers testifying to anything you wanted if you had the right currency: butter, eggs, cigarettes—especially American cigarettes—coffee. They shrugged me off.

"Kids can't go alone," they repeated.

"Why not?" I asked. "A family of one?"

"Kids can't go alone. That's the way it is!"

"But my papers are correct and signed!"

"Kids can't go alone," they repeated, apparently unimpressed.

"There is nothing like that in the regulations," I said. I hadn't read them, but I didn't think they had read them either. They were swamped with regulations.

"Huh, smart!" They gave me a mocking look and shouted, "Next!"

I asked for a superior official and was brushed aside. They pretended not to hear and went on questioning the people behind me.

"I will get one of the Russian guards to settle our dispute." I had raised my voice and started to open the door. It worked.

"Just a moment," they called. "That won't be necessary. We can make exceptions!"

Immediately I was held back. Suddenly the regulations were of no importance. I received my ticket and the appropriate car number and was almost bowed outside. I had scared them.

It had been a bluff. I would never have involved the guard. How could I have explained to him my predicament with the few words of Russian I had learned so far in school? What would he have done, totally confused by explanations and counterexplanations? Marched us all to his commanding officer? Or emptied his gun into the wall over our heads?

I clutched my ticket and shouldered my bag. People jammed the platform with mountains of their belongings and more flooded up the stairs every minute, their papers checked and stamped, escorted by relatives and friends. They squeezed through the waiting crowd. When the train pulled in, all hell broke loose.

It was a freight train. The doors of the boxcars were wide open and high above the platform. People stormed for the doors. They pressed forward relentlessly. They pushed and kicked and hit and punched one another. Kids were walked on and slapped aside. Luggage was thrown, slammed into backs, shoved against legs. They wrestled one another off the high stoops, tore one another out of the wagons. They fought for the wrong doors as often as not. The cars were poorly marked, sometimes not marked at all, and soon people were struggling out while others were forcing their way in.

Self-preservation kept me outside the battle. I knew I could not match any of the combatants in size or weight. So I stood well out of range and watched and waited till everybody and all their luggage were put aboard and only the people who had come along to see the transport off remained on the platform. Then I looked for the car assigned to me and tried to climb in.

They would not let me. Men and women had formed a solid circle around a wheelchair inside the doorway and blocked the entrance. No one moved aside for me and my bag. No one showed any interest in me. They were concerned about the wheelchair. It was using too much space—space they thought they needed to pile their bundles and stretch their legs. They wanted to get rid of the chair.

"It doesn't seem fair that some take up so much more room than others. We are all holding the same tickets, aren't we?" a woman in a black-and-white rabbit-fur coat said as she smiled into each face in the circle.

"I could use such a chair as much as the next person." The speaker, a red-haired man with one empty trouser leg folded up and pinned to his belt, knocked against the floor with his crutch and his neighbors nodded.

"There must be some rule prohibiting wheelchairs on crowded transports," a mousy man in glasses addressed himself to the circle. "Shouldn't we inform the stationmaster?"

"What do we need a stationmaster for? We should take things in our own hands," answered the red-haired man and again those around him nodded. To them it did not matter that a white-haired, frail, absolutely still person rested in the chair. It was too bad: if she could not travel without the chair, then she should be left behind. The old man next to her, frail and thin and white-haired himself, would not be able to prevent it. It was a miracle that he had managed to get the wheelchair into the car. In the confusion of boarding, someone must have helped him by mistake. Now nobody took his side, and the circle of men and women, hard-faced and ugly, were prepared to lift the chair down again and dump it on the platform with its occupant. It was a boy, twelve years old perhaps, who saved the old couple. He shouted and his voice broke with glee: "Tip the chair over! Throw them out!"

That startled the others, especially when his mother slapped him. Something like shame passed over their faces and they were suddenly eager to leave the old man and his wheelchair alone and turn to me as if nothing had happened.

I was still waving my ticket and holding up my bag to point out to them that I was provided with the same ticket, the same boxcar number as they—that I traveled alone, one child, thirteen and rather small for her age, pigtailed, wearing a skirt, jacket, and ankle boots, and carrying one piece of luggage. I did not plead, since I had just as much right as they to board the train.

And the same men and women who just a moment ago had been ready to chuck an old and helpless person off the train, tried to show themselves kindhearted and friendly. "There is always room for a kid!" exclaimed the red-haired man. "Hand us your bag!"

"You poor child!" clucked rabbit coat. "All alone and in these terrible times!"

"Let us help you," they called. They smiled and reached for me, patted my head and stroked my shoulder. They used me to cover up for their cruelty. I was not going along with them. I did not smile back; I brushed their hands off me and went over and leaned against the cold metal of the wheelchair, next to the open door, where the expected draft had kept the area relatively empty. Here the old man claimed me, placing a hand on my shoulder. I shook it off. I was not going to have anything to do with him either.

Then I sat and watched and listened. Every square foot of space was taken up by people and luggage, but some seemed a lot less cramped than others. The red-haired man—by now people were calling him captain—lounged on a mattress, and rabbit coat smiled from behind a wall of suitcases, while near them another woman with three small kids still did not know where to put the youngest. The mousy man had organized his family comfortably and a fat woman counted her bags and boxes.

There was no more talk about getting rid of anybody; now they complained about the transport. It was late already and there was no indication that it would depart soon. Also, it consisted of freight cars and they had understood they would be traveling in coaches. It was insulting to be forced to ride a freight train.

"Like cattle," cried the boy who had inadvertently rescued the old people, and threw straw into the air. He had a talent for emphasizing the worst, and again his mother boxed him behind the ears and told him to shut up.

He was right, though. We were penned in cattle cars and nobody had even bothered to sweep the floor. It was a disgrace. Where were the officials? The railroad clerks? The stationmaster? The conductors? Was nobody doing his work anymore? Order had collapsed with the defeat of the German Reich.

"Like cattle," fumed the mousy man. "It would not have happened before."

Yet I knew and they knew there had been millions

of people crammed into cattle cars during the war and before. We had seen pictures in school, in the newspapers, on the walls, in the streets, in the movie houses. Every single man, woman, and child in town had had to attend a documentary on the concentration camps or they would not have received their ration stamps and would have gone hungry.

You could avert your eyes quickly, but not fast enough, or close them and keep them closed. Yet behind the closed eyes the pictures were there: people herded into stations at gunpoint, many stations, everywhere in the country, even in your own town, and pushed and beaten into cattle cars by other people who were no different from you or your parents or your neighbors; hands reaching out of locked wagons, doomed faces behind wires. They were going to suffer death and they did not know it, yet they wore the signs of death on their faces.

There were pictures, too, that showed them dead. Naked, piled one on the other. And mountains of their belongings: shoes, clothing, hair, canes, dolls.

"Lies, lies," the teacher had mumbled in school, "nothing but propaganda. Wicked propaganda. We did not kill those people. They staged it."

"Vastly exaggerated," my father had said when I asked him about it. "Don't forget how many they killed when they bombed Dresden," and I never approached him about it again. My mother had turned away, silent.

Nobody was going to talk about it, but *I* knew, *they* knew. We all would carry those pictures with us the rest of our lives along with the names Auschwitz and Bergen Belsen and Treblinka.

Why didn't they shut up about cattle cars? Why didn't they? Nobody had forced them to board this transport. They should be glad they didn't have to walk back to Cologne. For months after the end of the war the trains had not run and now only a few were scheduled. With a special permit and after days of waiting you might be lucky enough to win a place on the roof or on the bumpers. Tracks were still in disrepair or else they had been removed and shipped to Russia as war reparations; coaches and freight cars had been bombed and burned or were on their way to the east. Travel inside the Russian zone was restricted, particularly across the border into the western zones. I had waited for this transport for many weeks. It had been postponed again and again. I had packed and unpacked a dozen times and gone my rounds to say good-by till it embarrassed me to be seen.

"I thought you had left long ago," people had said, as if I had already been counted out of their lives.

As the weeks dragged on, I had hoped at times that mother or father would change their minds about sending me to school near Cologne, a school they had never visited themselves. But mother had kept on talking about the advantages of my going there and had promised me a swift and uncomplicated trip. As if anything in the spring of 1946 could have been swift and uncomplicated or in any way predictable. For something as simple as a loaf of bread you had to stand in line for hours and often in vain; the many delays in the transport's departure had already proved her wrong. But she refused to admit it.

She wanted me to leave. So I did not beg her or father to be allowed to remain with them. I would leave, but I did not intend to go to their school. I was going to live alone and try to trace my brother Jochen, who had last written from a hospital in the west almost two years ago. I liked to imagine that I would discover what had happened to him after they cut his leg off. And perhaps I would find him alive . . .

"Are you really all by yourself?" Two of the women buttonholed me and looked me over.

I nodded.

"I am Frau Hasselmann and this is Frau Warnke." One presented the other. I had noticed them before: Frau Hasselmann was the mother of the outspoken boy, whom she slapped almost routinely every time he opened his mouth, and Frau Warnke had been sitting near the captain with her three kids, fenced in by other people's luggage.

"Are you going back to Cologne? To meet your parents? They must be worried. How can they let you travel alone?" Frau Hasselmann waited eagerly for an answer.

"They probably couldn't help it," put in Frau Warnke.

I glared at them, silent.

"We are going to keep an eye on you, for your mother's sake," announced Frau Hasselmann. "You will be in good hands."

"Perhaps we can help you," added Frau Warnke.

"I can take care of myself," I said coldly, but Frau Hasselmann did not listen.

"You can sit with Rudi and me." She pointed to her corner, from which Rudi observed our conversation and now stuck his tongue out in a form of greeting.

I shook my head vigorously. "No, thank you. I'd rather stay alone," I said and turned the other way. I wanted to remain independent.

"Did you hear that? That tone of voice?" grumbled Frau Hasselmann, and they both retreated. Yet later Frau Warnke sent one of her three kids over to make me join her group.

"Mother thinks you might like to be with us," said the boy and reached for my bag. I slapped his hand away.

"Tell her to leave me alone," I growled. I kept my place near the old man and the woman in the wheelchair. I didn't even dare to get off the car and march up and down the platform like most people. I was afraid they would not let me enter a second time. So I had sat and waited till 3:17 in the afternoon.

---3

NOW AS THE TRAIN made its way westward they glared at me: the kids jealous because I had nobody to tell me what to do and what not to do; Frau Warnke and Frau Hasselmann outraged because I had rejected their company; the others because I took up space and was somehow mixed up with the old couple and the wheelchair, which took up more space.

I glared back.

There was no room anywhere, so why not stay right where I was, at the open door? The old man had secured my bag behind the wheelchair during the rush in and now pushed it over to me. I thanked him with a smile, half for him, half for the old woman. But she did not pay attention to me. Instead, she lay quite still and her wide-open eyes watched far more interesting events in the distance, events she would not share with anyone else. Her face was white and the air puffed in and out of her slightly opened mouth in an audible hiss. Breathing like that gets you awfully thirsty. Perhaps the old man had forgotten to pack something to drink.

"Would you like some lemonade?" I offered my bottle. It was still full and I could afford to share some of it. But would he understand that not all was meant for him?

He reached for the bottle and I watched rather anxiously as he unscrewed it with trembling hands. As he bent back to swallow a mouthful, he closed his red-rimmed eyes and the Adam's apple moved up and down in his thin and withered neck. He only took one small mouthful, then he carefully wiped the top of the bottle with his sleeve and handed it back with a smile. Relieved, I smiled back. I liked his kind of smile. It broke up the lines of worry and sadness and made him glow with friendliness.

"Would she?" I gestured toward the wheelchair.

"My wife, Mrs. Lauritzen? It would do her good, but I am afraid she does not want a drink right now. I do thank you for your kindness."

I almost asked him what was wrong with her, but

he had turned to her and was talking softly before I could open my mouth. I was glad, because it was really none of my business and I knew I would not like it at all if he asked me a lot of questions. We were strangers who just happened to be pushed next to each other.

So I drank most of my lemonade. It was already late in the afternoon and I had missed lunch waiting for our departure. Breakfast had been a long time ago and not exactly filling either. Suddenly I felt terribly hungry and inspected my food supply.

It was not much, but fortunately more than one would ordinarily pack for a day's ride: two pounds of potato salad with some fake mayonnaise in a container that could be used for soups, stews, tea, or anything else that the railroad stations or soup kitchens might dish out; four slices of dry bread and at least another two pounds of imitation flavored candy.

That accounted for more than a month's ration of sugar and two-day's ration of bread. The potatoes had come from the black market; we had traded them for our living-room rug only three weeks ago.

I was rich.

I knew there was no chance we would arrive in Cologne by night as scheduled, so I thought I should economize with my food and try to spread the supply through the long hours ahead—perhaps even save a bit for my new start alone. So I allowed myself half the potato salad. I remembered that it spoiled quickly in the summer and, though it was only April and not very warm outside, the people crowded in the car together had raised the temperature inside considerably.

It tasted good, but salty, so I drank the rest of the lemonade. There should be water somewhere along the line to refill the bottle.

Some were richer. The fat woman caressed a hard-boiled egg, peeled it slowly, and swallowed it whole. And the captain bit into a piece of sausage and drank from a dark bottle and his face turned as red as his hair. He belched.

I picked some candy for dessert and saw Rudi and the Warnke kids watching me. Had they been watching me all along and counting my supplies? Did they think I would share my food with them?

I decided to tease them. I asked Mr. Lauritzen politely if he cared for some candy. He answered just as politely that he would love a piece and he fished one out of my box and wrapped it carefully in a piece of newspaper and stored it in his pocket. Only then did I fold four pieces of candy into a scrap of paper and toss it over to Rudi and bury my box deep into the bag.

"Thank you," shouted Rudi, and his mother smacked him for being so loud. Maybe I should have offered my candy to her or the fat woman or the captain, rabbit coat or the mousy guy, to people who were obviously more important in our boxcar.

Then I sat in the open door and dangled my legs outside. The train was rolling along rather slowly and I held onto a bar, so it was far from dangerous. But I knew that my parents would have made a terrible fuss and would have ordered me away from the door and that many of the people behind me—the adults, not the kids—itched to give a similar order. If one had started to speak, the others would have joined immediately in scolding me. Yet they would not care if I fell off so long as I did not involve them.

Frau Hasselmann talked loudly about bringing up children and how some people seemed to fail. "Discipline! It all depends on discipline!" she exclaimed. "I do not spare the rod if necessary."

I could not hear Frau Warnke's remark, only Frau Hasselmann's answer. "Spare the rod and spoil the child!" she said, her voice sharp.

I gave them a frosty look. I was free.

I stayed at the open door even though it was getting rather cold, and the rushing wind blew through my jacket and my blouse and my undershirt and I shivered. I dangled my legs and wiggled my toes and admired my ankle-high boots, which were made with the best leather. "Peacetime quality," my mother had said with a sigh, and though we had had peace for over a year now, it apparently was not the right kind of peace. You wouldn't be able to get leather like that anywhere. I dreaded the time I would outgrow the boots. How could I ever replace them? They were a little tight already and Wolfgang was waiting to inherit them. Father never really explained where he got the leather in the winter of '44/'45. Strange that one could find anything of peacetime quality after five years of war. But I was lucky that it had not been enough leather for a pair of shoes for him or mother. I flexed my feet and the shoes easily bent with them. How uncomfortable it would be to have to wear shoes with wooden soles again.

We had passed a couple of small towns and villages

and now I could see a larger town surrounded by its medieval walls and towers and gates, all built in red brick and miraculously overlooked in the bombing. The sun hit the church towers and they saluted back in green copper flashes.

We pulled into a huge station and the train grunted to a stop and pushed off a second later without giving us an opportunity to fetch water or search for a restroom. How angry the people were! I would have liked a bottle of water myself. And three platforms away a dripping faucet was in clear view! You could not even scream at the stationmaster; the station was deserted.

It had been an important station, but it was obsolete now. Trains that used to pass through to cities in the west no longer ran. The town almost straddled the border between the Russian and British zones and this particular part had been sealed for a month, at least to trains. People on foot were said to cross all the time, some legally and many illegally. This took a lot of time because you had to creep through woods and keep out of the sight of soldiers.

The four different armies that occupied Germany watched over their borders jealously and in their zones they made the people sing their songs, greet their flags, and follow their laws; the kids had to learn their language. People soon said the American zone was the most comfortable to live in, mainly because they liked Virginia cigarettes better than the French Gauloises or the Russian Machorka or the British Players. Also Russian and French were a lot more difficult to learn than English. Especially Russian.

I don't pretend to understand why it was so important to prevent people from leaving the zones—perhaps they feared that everybody would go after American cigarettes or that every German would suddenly decide that he wanted to learn Russian—but the French, the British, the Americans, and the Russians all kept their borders locked and guarded except for a few crossings and made it quite tedious to get permissions to visit in another zone, let alone to relocate.

Therefore we had to turn south till we reached one of the official holes in the border. Later I realized that if I had jumped the train with my bag and walked for not more than two hours, I would have arrived in the British zone, where I could have caught a different train for Cologne. I might have reached Cologne five days before the transport. *Five days!* But I didn't know that then, and I was too scared to cross the border by myself. What if I walked in the wrong direction? Or right into a Russian or British guard? So I sat and watched the countryside.

The walls and towers disappeared and again we rode through woods and fields, untended, brown, and weedy. We rode alongside placid lakes and through villages. Then the country changed steadily. The beeches gave way to pines and birch, the soil became sandy and light, the fields were replaced by meadows. Firepaths were cut into the woods. The land was empty: nowhere was there a town, village, or even a house.

The wood opened into a vast plain, almost treeless, and violet with heather. The train crawled, braked, crawled a few more yards, and braked to a complete stop.

"What the hell is going on?" shouted the captain, and stuck his red face out the door. "What are they thinking of now?"

Everyone crammed into the doorway to find out what was going on. They shouted inquiries along the train line, but no answers came back from the engine. They must have heard us up front, but they ignored our questions. Rabbit coat leaned heavily against me to see outside and I jumped onto the embankment under her pressure. There I heard the click.

It was a faint metallic click, almost inaudible in the clamor, and while I wondered if it was important, I saw a figure emerge between the engine and the first car and mount the locomotive. The whistle sounded, steam blew up with great force, and the engine moved forward. But *we* didn't: they had disconnected it from the transport.

People inside did not realize yet what was happening. "Come back in, or you will be left behind!" urged Frau Warnke.

"Don't worry," I said. "It's easy to get back in."

The captain barred the doorway with his crutch and laughed at his own prank: "Then we have to make it more difficult!"

The whistle blew once more. The engine was steaming down the track.

4

PEOPLE POURED OUT OF the cars and we followed the engine with our eyes, unbelieving. It could not be true! Any moment she must stop and reverse herself. Yet she steamed down the single track, farther and farther away, and melted into the dark band of a distant forest. When she had vanished completely, screams of fury and anger arose. Again people searched for someone responsible. A conductor, a clerk! But the transport had been stranded without anyone in command. There was nobody to explain our situation, nobody to tell us where we were and when the engine would return, nobody to tell us what to do.

The transport, with fifteen freight cars full of evacuees, was marooned on an open heath somewhere four hours away from the district capital with no town or village in sight. And night was falling quickly. It was hard to accept and everybody took precautions and stayed close to the train or even inside, refusing to believe that they had been abandoned for the time being. They watched the sky for signs of smoke and listened for the whistle and the sounds of the engine.

At first I wandered about more or less alone. I had seen something that looked like a building, half-hidden behind clumps of birches, and decided to investigate. Wouldn't it be great if I could find water before anyone else started to search for it? Not only could I drink—and I was certainly thirsty enough—but I would be the hero of the evening. We all needed water.

Nevertheless I felt quite anxious about leaving the train so far behind and I stumbled more than twice over large lumps of heather because my eyes were glued to the track. There was always the possibility that the engine would return though I thought it quite unlikely. Not tonight.

The building was a cottage, deserted and half in ruin. The windows were broken, the roof caved sideways, and the door was missing. Still, I hoped for water and stepped inside into the gloom. I saw a table, a bench, a bed, a cupboard with two chipped beer mugs, a wood stove. It must have been a hunter's shelter. How stupid of me to look for a faucet with running water, as if we were in the middle of town. I backed out and circled the cottage. Between black junipers stood the pump.

It looked rusty and dead. I grabbed the handle and the hinges squeaked. The whole pump shrieked pitifully across the plain as if the sudden action hurt. I pumped up and down and up and down and listened for the gurgle of water deep inside. I thought I heard a murmur and pumped quicker, when a weight held the handle and out burst a stream of water.

Real water!

Someone pushed me aside, snatched the handle away, and continued pumping. The water gushed forward in a steady flow.

"I found water!" cried the mousy man." I found a pump and it's working fine." His voice, high-pitched with glee and excitement, carried back to the train. Soon he was surrounded by half the transport. People slapped his back and told him how smart he was and what would they do without him. Nobody took notice of me. The mousy man assumed control; he ordered people to form a line, he organized crews to pump and distribute the water. I bet he would have loved to issue ration cards. U. S. 1821644

I had to queue up like everybody else. At my pump.

"I found the water," I told Mr. Lauritzen and anybody else who cared to listen. "I thought of it first and I discovered the pump and then this mousy man, you know the one from our car who always talks about regulations, pushes me aside and claims he found the water."

"Not many people remember who built the cathedral in Cologne," said Mr. Lauritzen.

"But that's different! It happened such a long time ago. Besides, I bet people knew who built the cathedral at the time he was building it," I insisted. "Tell me, who was it?"

Suddenly Mr. Lauritzen was very busy rummaging in his bag. Apparently he could not find what he was looking for. He straightened up again, faced me squarely, and said: "I don't know," and he blushed. Then we both laughed.

"Would you like some water?" I asked.

"Yes, please." he said. "Could you get me some of your water?"

The sun had set and the sky had changed from blue to yellowish-green to gray to night blue. Darkness spread quickly and people withdrew into their cars, where a few candles flickered. Here they ate and drank in their own groups and gulped their food down silently. Only the fat woman annoyed everyone by smacking her lips. What was she eating? It sounded as if she sucked the meat off a bone. Mr. Lauritzen gnawed a dry crust of bread and Mrs. Lauritzen held her eyes open and breathed in louder puffs and neither ate nor drank.

I swallowed most of my potato salad and could easily have cleaned it all up, but the prospect of a long day on four slices of dry bread—we had at least seven more hours to travel to reach Cologne—worried me enough to save some for tomorrow. Someone started a fire outside and I leaped out immediately to help collect dry branches and armfuls of heather. Soon three big fires flared. The fat woman called for tea, but it was too dark to gather dried leaves. One might pick the wrong kind. We should have thought of it earlier.

People flocked around the fires, the children laughed and threw bits and pieces of wood into the flames, and I laughed with them. Rudi and I went for more wood and we gave the Warnke kids torches and lighted them and danced around. It felt warm and comfortable to be together. The fires were beautiful, the night still, the stars luminous above.

Stories began to go around, scary stories about trains just like ours, abandoned somewhere in the countryside and then attacked by marauding soldiers who killed those who tried to defend themselves and robbed and looted the baggage. People whispered about what had happened to the women and girls;

they hinted about rape and mutilation. Everyone knew it had happened and it could happen again.

Terrified, the people extinguished the fires; they pulled the flaming branches apart and stamped on the hot coals and stole into the cars. They barricaded the doors and just minutes later the transport stood silent and apparently deserted on the plain.

They had terrified me too and I had crept along with them. I had helped to block and secure our door before rabbit coat blew out the candle. Now I felt trapped behind the locked door. It was no protection. It was ridiculous to feel safe behind it. I knew it as well as anybody else. *They* would order us to open it and we would obey. How could we defend ourselves against guns?

I shuddered. It was tempting to crawl over and join Frau Hasselmann and Rudi or the Warnkes, just to be close to somebody and to whisper in Rudi's ear or the Warnke kids', but I knew they would not let me go tomorrow if I surrendered now. So I crouched and pressed my face against the door and saw a star through a tiny slit in the wood and smelled the cold smoke of our dead fires. I listened.

We had not thought of posting guards, so there was nobody to warn us. In our flight to hide we had behaved stupidly. Now everybody listened to the night, tense with fear. Some of the smaller kids began to cry and were harshly told to cut it out. They continued to sob into their sleeves. The old people smothered their coughs in shawls and pillows. Only Mrs. Lauritzen, oblivious to any danger, breathed loudly and coughed her dry, unrestrained coughs.

Minute after minute dragged on. I cursed myself

for creeping aboard with the others, for seeking refuge with them. I wanted to break out of this prison, I wanted to be able to run and run if the soldiers came. How I wished I had stayed outside. Now I was caught in a trap.

I had hated the air-raid shelters, the bunkers and cellars that confined you. Wolfgang and I used to run away from the house at the first wail of the siren and hide in the woods whenever we could. We ran from the school, from the streets; the air raid warden had shouted after us and ordered us to stop. We ran on. We knew he could shoot us—they were supposed to shoot looters, and everybody who stayed above ground during an air raid was a looter—but we were far more frightened of being shut in.

We had felt that way ever since the bombs had buried us in the cellar of Kekenmeister's hardware store at the district capital one afternoon on the way home from the dentist. He had pulled two teeth from both of us and it almost had not been necessary. Eight people had been killed in the same cellar; the blast had thrown them into one corner, Wolfgang and me into the other. When they dug us up, we still clutched our bloody teeth . . .

I wanted to be outside—desperately. But how could I open the door? My throat felt tight and I pressed my face against the wood and thought of home.

5

me to leave. She had said I should go to a school near
Cologne, a boarding school one of her cousins had
stayed at before the war. She had said I would be
better off in one of the western zones—were not the
Americans rich?—and I would get more to eat. That's
what everybody said. At least I would get what the
ration cards said I was supopsed to get: meat for
meat stamps, eggs for egg stamps, sugar for sugar
stamps. In the western zones they did not substitute
cottage cheese for meat, a yellow powder for eggs,
an unidentifiable paste for butter. Their bread was
bread and not a mixture of straw, potatoes, cereal,
and floor sweepings. It was rumored that nobody in
the western zones was hungry and she wanted to
believe it. But if it was really that great, why didn't
everybody leave? Cross the border illegally? Buy
forged papers on the black market and be repatriated
to Munich or Bremerhaven? Why didn't she and
father and Wolfgang go with me?

Mother also said that without me there would be
one less mouth to feed, although she forgot that they
automatically would receive one less ration card. And
it was I who stood in line for everything at the stores.

And it was I who organized all—or almost all—our extra food. I had collected wild vegetables and mushrooms and berries and nuts and cereal. Who was going to do my job? Mother and father both worked; Wolfgang was easily squeezed out of queues and he picked inedible mushrooms and bitter greens. I did not correct her, though it hurt me that she never considered my work at home. I knew quite well she wanted me out of the house because of father.

Since he had come home from the war, partly disabled and without his real job, he and I had fought constantly. First we fought about words. He was not interested in what I did; he did not notice my friends or care about my schoolwork, but he scrutinized every word I said. He was looking for disrespect and he sensed it in every single remark I made. He flew into a rage when he thought his authority was being challenged and he twisted what I said. If I remained mute, he needled me continuously, as if he *wanted* an impertinent answer.

Then that was not enough. At least once a week he would beat me up. He would burst into a rage and knock me around violently. He would hit me with his clenched fists on my head, shoulders, arms, back: the blows fell everywhere. His wounded hand did not hamper him, though that arm was weaker than the other. Later I would try to figure out what had set him off. Which of my words? What tone of voice? What expression on my face? What had provoked him? There was no pattern, and I came to think that it was not really me he was hitting at.

It was a game, though I did not see what purpose it

served. It had nothing to do with me; Wolfgang could have been his partner or mother or Jochen, if he had been home. I just happened to be chosen and my so-called disrespect was only a pretext for his fury.

I must confess it did frighten me sometimes. Especially if he held me cornered and hammered blindly. It frightened mother, too. Several times she hurled herself between us to defend me and cried: "You are going to kill her! You are going to kill her!" Or she tried to hold his arms or pull him back, clutching his jacket.

He did not want to kill me. It had nothing to do with me. When it was over, he slumped on the couch, tired and spent, and hid behind his newspaper. I almost felt sorry for him then. He didn't understand the game either.

I thought of it as one more of the many incomprehensible things I had seen people do. Mother breaking into hysterical tears if one overslept the air-raid siren and therefore—half in dreams—refused to go into the cellar. Our school principal, Rektor Bolsenkoetter, shooting his family and himself before the Russians came and forgetting Albert, his youngest son, who was over playing with us. When we brought him home, we saw the blood dripping down the front steps and onto the sidewalk and they made me look in first. Or Miss Cecilia Jensen, who kept her black boots on when she washed herself naked before a mirror. Jochen on his last furlough had told us as a going-away present that one could watch her through the attic window. Usually on Saturday nights.

I did not hate father for hitting me, but I did hate

his constant complaints and the way he acted. Till the war ended he loafed around the house and talked about how we would win it with the new secret super weapons. He griped about a lukewarm soup or a smoking stove, the indolence of the plumber, who had not greeted him properly, and how fast the weeds grew in the garden. He never lifted a finger to help and excused himself with a terrible pain in his shoulder when the potatoes had to be picked, when the ashes had to be carried down, when the roof needed fixing, when the streets had to be swept Wednesdays and Saturdays, or even when the doorbell rang and someone had to answer.

"My shoulder hurts," he used to say. "What can you do with a hand that has two fingers missing?"

I could have told him.

So when the Russians came and put him to work, ignoring his hand and his shoulder and Dr. Ruff's certificate from which he had scratched the swastika, and he raked and weeded and planted their preposterous star-shaped, red-edged flower beds, I went out of my way and secretly watched him. I had come to laugh, but it suddenly was not funny at all. I don't think I felt sorry for him, only angry about all our lives.

Such forced labor naturally did not improve his disposition. He complained more and did not need a pretext to fly into a rage. Mother had reason to be worried and so she wanted us separated. Somehow she must have thought his outbursts were my fault because she proposed the boarding school near Cologne. Or was it easier to remove me from the family?

Perhaps she needed him and she did not need me? After a while she made no more effort to keep peace at home and only talked about the school.

I had read all about such schools in books from Ohlsen's library and they bored me: you spoke French and wore white gloves and poured tea from silver teapots and had refined adventures and gushy friendships. I had never owned white gloves and they appeared more than silly to me. How could you wash them without soap? We got one piece a month and it lasted no more than ten days. And what good are gray-white gloves? Why not woolen mittens to keep you warm? I didn't think much of their adventures and friendships either, though I admired the tea with its crumpets—whatever they were—and the cakes and cucumber sandwiches and jams and jellies and hot rolls.

But I had not objected. If she wanted me out of the house, I was ready to leave. Though I felt hurt. And I was going to miss Wolfgang and mother and perhaps even father and the house and my friends and the streets of the town and the fields and woods —even the long lines at the stores. I was going to miss it all.

Nevertheless I had decided to cut loose completely. They could keep their school. I was not going to swap father's demands for respect for somebody else's. Tea or no tea, they might be just as bothered about their authority as he was. I planned to stay on my own. I would be free and independent with nobody to tell me what to do and nobody to care for. I was finished with all that. Perhaps one day I would write to them;

perhaps one day I would find Jochen. The two of us could start fresh again.

I must have sighed. A bony hand stroked over my hair. I remembered my candy, pressed some in Mr. Lauritzen's hand, and filled my own mouth.

"I sold candy in my store too," whispered Mr. Lauritzen, "besides the bread and rice and noodles, soup mixes and dried peas and beans, cans with vegetables and oil, cakes of soap and Persil and other things." He paused and I imagined a store like the one at the corner of Linderstrasse and Weidenallee with its neat rows of shelves, a cash register that was always open because Frau Moenckemoeller liked to keep the money handy in a glass jar, and a faded yellow-and-red display for baking soda.

"We had two low boards with jars and boxes," Mr. Lauritzen went on and he sounded happy and content —he must have liked his life behind the counter, "strings of licorice, lemon drops, raspberries, buttery caramels, chocolate-covered pillows of foam, jelly eggs at Easter time, Santa Clauses in shiny wrappers. Mrs. Lauritzen made it a habit to reward each child with a sweet when they did errands for their mothers. We used up all our rations this way. Mrs. Lauritzen couldn't stop giving candy to the children. We—"

"Quiet," someone hissed angrily.

I wished he could go on telling me about the store. Did he and Mrs. Lauritzen have to drink their tea without sugar? Did they ever sell candy necklaces? Father had bought one for me many, many years ago, when I had walked home with him from work. I had kept it in a cigar box all this time and gave it to Wolfgang when I left. I could not take it along. I sucked my candy hard till the inside of my mouth was raw and painful.

6

RABBIT COAT STEPPED on my foot and woke me up.

"What a night! My legs feel dead."

"At last it's over," cried the captain. "Open the doors!"

"I thought about locking ourselves in," said the mousy man. "I am sure it was illegal. What would we have done in case of fire?"

"Fire! Fire!" cried Rudi. "Let's start one!"

"I would give anything for a cup of tea," moaned the fat woman and cradled the softest-looking pillow to her chest.

"I will get it, I'll get it," I called to her, wondering what that "anything" might be.

They opened the door, and the pale and still sunless sky painted our faces gray. All around people stretched arms and legs and yawned and lowered themselves stiffly from the cars down to the embankment and disappeared behind bushes and bunches of heather.

The tracks were empty in both directions and the plain peaceful. I ran up to my pump. My mouth was killing me and in the light of the early morning it seemed stupid and senseless to have eaten so much precious candy. The mousy man was hard at work. A long line waited already and he gave his orders. When my turn came, I drank and drank to blot the fire in my mouth.

Around me people filled pots and pans and pails and bottles and drank. They splashed water in their faces and gurgled and spit with relish. The night had passed without incident and now they were cheerful. The sky turned brighter too, and the first rays of sunlight swept over the heather, repainted its dark and gloomy colors, and retouched our faces.

I felt happy and carried water for all who needed it. I fetched wood for the cooking fire in front of our boxcar. I picked dry leaves—blackberry and a touch of rosemary—and brewed tea in Mr. Lauritzen's pot, tea of a beautiful golden color which I sweetened with pieces of my candy. Wild-cherry flavor.

The fat woman gave me a piece of bread with molasses in return for the tea and peeled herself another egg. There were already three other steaming cups at her side. The captain laughed and grabbed one and said something about our duty to the poor war veterans. Mr. Lauritzen drank a lot and Mrs. Lauritzen drank a little and sighed and coughed and closed her eyes. He wrapped the blanket around her.

It promised to be a fair day, windless, cloudless, warm.

One after another, people boarded the transport and settled inside. We waited for the engine. Surely she would return any minute and we would travel on. Already we were a day behind schedule. We waited and waited and nothing happened, absolutely nothing. I scanned the horizon: there was no steam or smoke, the track remained idle and only the sun climbed higher in the sky.

It was boring. So I jumped out again without anybody's permission and behind me heard Rudi nag and the Warnke kids ask for more water. Not long after, their mothers relented and allowed them out too because by now everybody had spilled out again and the grownups were gathered in angry groups.

The kids played games to pass the time: hopscotch in sandy spots, hide-and-seek in the heather and among the junipers. I threw rocks at targets and competed with Rudi and beat him easily. He was a lousy pitcher and a sore loser and shouted that I had been cheating and that anyway there must be something wrong with me—why else would my parents let me travel alone at a time like this—and that his mother thought so too. The other kids gloated.

"My parents are dead," I called back and walked to the wagon. Only the Lauritzens had stayed inside.

"Why don't you come out in the sun?" I asked. "It's beautiful."

"Well"—Mr. Lauritzen hesitated—"it's the wheelchair. I fear I won't get it back in alone and Mrs. Lauritzen can't be without it." So he was still convinced that the people would try to leave him behind deliberately, and maybe he was right. Especially if there were another rush.

"I promise to help you. I am strong enough," I said. I thought it quite unpleasant for anybody to be stuck in the car all day, and the sun might even heal Mrs.

Lauritzen's strange, dry cough. I would even help rabbit coat or the mousy man get out if they asked me. So we lifted the chair down together and wheeled it into a protected spot and I offered to guard Mrs. Lauritzen while the old man walked back and forth restlessly.

"I am sure we will be in Cologne tonight," I said to her, but she paid no attention to me. "You know," I whispered close to her face, "my papers are false. We bought them for butter and eggs. I never saw Cologne in my whole life!" Her face showed no reaction. I listened to her laborious breathing. We had been close together for twenty-four hours and all during that time she had hardly moved. I had not heard her speak, nor had she eaten or drunk anything but the mouthful of tea an hour ago. I wondered if she was very sick or just old and tired and weary. What did she see when she looked straight through me? Her face was wrinkled all over and she had two hairy warts on one cheek. Her lips were thin and sunken and trembled with each breath. Her white hair, tinged with yellow, was covered by a shawl. Sometimes it seemed as if she smiled and I always smiled back.

Why did she travel? Why would Mr. Lauritzen travel with her? Why was he going to Cologne under such circumstances? Why didn't he wait till she was well? Perhaps his papers were as false as mine and he had invented the grocery store as I had invented a street and school for myself in Cologne, and he had only told me his story for practice. Perhaps they were running away in disguise: he had bleached his hair and she was faking her illness. Perhaps they were wanted by the police, here or in another country. Wanted for war crimes. There were thousands of war criminals. And practically anybody was suspect: generals and all the military, party officials, members of lots of different organizations.

In my town the mayor, the chief of the party, the chief of police, and Karstens, the owner of the mill, were supposed to be war criminals, the more important ones. The mayor and the two chiefs had fled and were hiding somewhere, but Karstens had been hung from the chestnut in front of his house by the Polish and French prisoners of war, who had worked at the mill. They drank and sang a lot the night they hung Karstens and for a week nobody was allowed to cut him down. I saw him myself on the way to school.

I searched Mrs. Lauritzen's face for traces of a mask, but it looked real and far away and I almost apologized for my thoughts.

"Where is your store in Cologne? Why did you leave it?" I questioned Mr. Lauritzen when he came back.

"Hofweg 19," he replied. "It burned down not long after we left. If they had allowed us to stay, I could have extinguished the fire, I am sure. Three pails of sand we kept in the hall. But they had their regulations." He shrugged his shoulders and I knew as much as before. Everybody kept three pails of sand in the hall and one pail of water and a broom for beating out the flames.

Then he chuckled. "We turned the ration coupons over to them in an incredible muddle! One drawer full of bits and pieces of different colored paper! Mrs.

Lauritzen and I did not like the work of gluing them on sheets of paper, so we always waited till the very last moment. And they were due a day after our departure. You should have seen their faces!" He beamed at me and I felt sheepish about my suspicion. Anyway, if he had anything to hide it was no concern of mine.

I wormed my way into the center of a large group to listen to what they had to say. They did not know when the engine would return; they did not know if food would be delivered.

"Impossible situation," they said.

"It's incredible," they said. "Twenty-four hours like this and no end in sight!"

"It would never have happened, if . . ." and others nodded.

"We had order," they said.

"Do you think they would let us starve to death here? I haven't a bite to eat!"

Why doesn't somebody walk up to the next town and ask what is going to happen to us? I wanted to shout. But they do not listen to anyone my age. So I looked for one of the Warnke kids—their mother seemed a lot nicer to them than Frau Hasselmann was to Rudi—and told him to tell his mother as sort of his own idea and soon Frau Warnke squeezed into the middle of the group and proposed my plan: a delegation should be sent to inquire after our fate. After all, men, women, and children had been left stranded for more than twelve hours.

"I would volunteer immediately," said rabbit coat, "but who would look after my family?" Her daughter looked thirty to me.

"You need someone faster than me." The captain lifted his crutch. I noticed he had skipped to the pump many times and demanded his place at the head of the line. He skipped faster than other people could walk.

"I really haven't the strength," sighed a plump woman. "I haven't eaten in such a long time."

It was only when Frau Warnke said she would go herself and take her three kids along that people grumbled, saying that she would be too slow, and three others stepped forward.

"We will go right up to the commandant," they shouted as they marched off under our cheers. I did not believe them. In my town everybody made wide detours around the office of the commandant, the seat of the highest military official—everybody but small kids and Russian soldiers. These people too would lose their courage along the way and at most confront a German railroad clerk and not the Russian commandant. And who could blame them! They would be told, if there was hope, that the transport would continue, or else they would come back with the advice to pack up and walk back to where we came from.

In the last days of the war a trainful of wounded soldiers and people fleeing from East Prussia had arrived at the station in my town and never moved on. I had walked through the crowd each day in my uniform of the Hitler Youth and poured hot substitute coffee—another of my efforts to help us win the war—and each day there were fewer people. Some left on foot; others hitched rides on a truck or an ambulance; some transferred into our crowded hospital; some died. After ten days the coaches were almost vacant and we played cards with the five soldiers who had set up housekeeping with the stuff the refugees had left behind. It was cozy in there between our rounds of pouring coffee on the windy platform, and I won one iron cross first class, the epaulets of a general, and sealed orders to a Colonel Bellen to return immediately to his outfit in Kiev.

But now it should be different. There must be other trains stacked up behind us—if we were on the main line. I was not particularly worried. The rest of the potato salad would serve as lunch, half of the bread would do for dinner, and the other half for breakfast. The pump was working well. There was tea to brew, sweetened with candy. If the fat woman peeled another hard-boiled egg, I would refuse to watch.

Too bad the season was wrong to find anything edible outside. Too early for mushrooms or green vegetables, dandelions or stinging nettles, watercress or the nutty seedlings of beeches. Perhaps I would look for bird's nests and their eggs, or dried berries and last year's nuts. It was so much more fun to collect wild foods than to check the stores.

I used to queue up for hours at the slightest hint that bread might be sold, or cooking oil, margarine, or sugar. At first I had some trouble keeping my place in line. People tried to push me out of it or sneaked around me, and some claimed loudly that I was trying to get ahead while they squeezed in ahead of me. Older women behaved the worst: they treated kids as if we lined up for pure pleasure and they walked to the head of the queue and the shopkeepers sided with them.

"It doesn't hurt young legs to stand a little longer."
(How about our chances to get a loaf of bread before the supply ran out?)

"They have nothing better to do!"

I wondered if mother and father pushed kids aside. After some experience I learned to fight for my place. I stepped on feet, kicked if necessary, pushed rudely, and talked back, but I never liked it.

Gathering wild foods was different and I had been proud of my success in supplementing our rations. I had ground the cereal, canned the vegetables, dried the fruit and mushrooms, and raised rabbits with Wolfgang's help.

How would they live without me? Well, that was their business now. I could not help them, so I put it out of my mind.

I was not worried, but Mr. Lauritzen looked drawn and distressed when I reported what had been decided. Mrs. Lauritzen coughed in spite of the warm sun.

"Time is running out," he said, and I had no idea what he was talking about. "We can't wait much longer." He spoke more to himself than to me. Then with his eyes he measured me from head to toe. "Will you help me?" he asked.

"Sure," I said. Hadn't I helped him before? "The wheelchair is no problem. Shall we get it back in now?"

"That's not quite what I mean," he said, but right then Rudi called and I excused myself to lead an excursion into the field, so I missed my chance to find out what he meant.

"Mother told me to be nice to you," Rudi grinned. "Because you are an orphan."

7

"THEY'RE COMING, THEY'RE coming!"

It was late afternoon when three figures appeared on the tracks and trudged slowly closer. We raced to greet them. How tired they looked! They brushed us off and did not answer our questions. They waited till they were surrounded by other grownups.

"Nothing," they said. "And how we tried!"

"We walked all the way to Sandhagen, twelve miles!"

"They do not have an engine and they can not send one."

"Ours? It steamed through Sandhagen without stopping!"

"They want the line cleared, too. There are three trains piled behind us."

"When? Tomorrow! They promised! Early tomorrow morning!"

"They are doing what they can."

"The office of the commandant? No! Are you kidding?"

"Well, you could have gone yourself. Nobody tried to hold you back!"

"Besides, they warned us. He is a Tartar. Ever met one of those?"

"Food? They have nothing to spare in Sandhagen."

"Food? Perhaps tomorrow on the way."

"Soldiers? No danger there. That's what they think at the station. Nothing to worry about, thank goodness."

"Why are we left here? We *lost* that goddamned war!"

Mr. Lauritzen trembled when I told him what I had heard. "Tomorrow may be too late," he said and wrapped Mrs. Lauritzen more tightly in her blanket. Her face hardly showed between the shawl and the gray cover, and she rasped painfully.

"Too late for what?" I asked, curious. "I will make more tea and you could have half of my potato salad if you have nothing left to eat."

"Too late for Mrs. Lauritzen," he said and fidgeted with the blanket. "I have to get her home."

"But we will be in Cologne tomorrow," I insisted, "and nobody is going to throw you off the transport now."

"You promised to help me," said the old man and again measured me from head to toe. I felt uneasy under his scrutiny. Hadn't I lifted the wheelchair before? What was he getting at?

But he must have meant he needed my help to get back into our boxcar because he steered toward it, and I wheeled the chair and together we heaved it inside. I promised to bring tea for the evening meal.

I collected choice blackberry leaves and fetched water. I brewed tea and carried it back to the boxcar. I reached for my candy to sweeten it, but the candy was gone. Stolen!

Practically everyone in our whole car had had the

opportunity to steal it. Everyone could have seen me offer the box to the old man and then store it in my bag. Rudi and the Warnke kids, Frau Hasselmann, Frau Warnke, the captain, the fat woman, rabbit coat, any of the others.

I was so furious I could have kicked the thief. I found and kicked Rudi and he kicked me back and swore he had taken nothing. He showed his tongue, and it was just a normal tongue, pink with white spots and without the telltale signs of artificial coloration. My candy would have dyed his mouth green and purple and yellow and blue for hours.

One after the other I forced the Warnke kids to open their mouths and stick out their tongues and they too proved their innocence. They looked at me as if I had gone crazy. There was nothing else I could do, since I could not think of any practical way to make the fat woman or the other people show their tongues to me. And the tea was cold now.

"Mrs. Lauritzen once believed a shipment of chocolate hearts was stolen," said Mr. Lauritzen. "When actually they had dropped into the barrel with pickled herring. And we almost accused Walter. After their vinegar bath we could not even give them away, and the herring tasted sort of strange too. Some customers wondered about it."

He fished out of his pocket the candy that I had given him yesterday. "Lucky I forgot all about it."

So I brewed a new pot of tea and we shared it. The artificial lemon mixed well with the blackberry and I was glad he had not chosen fake licorice. Mrs. Lauritzen drank very little.

Later the fires flared high. There was talk of keeping them alive all night. Why should we be hungry and cold and cramped, the people asked. Their fear of marauding soldiers was forgotten. I worked hard. I went far out into the plain and pulled big loads of dead wood. And Rudi and I secured boards from the roof of the cottage and hauled two chairs from inside. We built our own fire and waved torches. Then we sat and watched the flames. One by one the children were called inside and told to sleep. Nobody called me. I stayed with the fire and dozed off. At least I must have closed my eyes.

When I opened them again, the fires burned low and people huddled in sleep around them. I don't know what made me get up and walk over to my box-car. Did I hear a call? I put my head inside the half-closed door and listened.

"Get some water! Quick, quick!" It was Mr. Lauritzen's voice, low and urgent.

I grabbed the pot and ran. The pump shrieked through the night and people stirred uneasily when I passed the fires. I climbed inside the car. Mr. Lauritzen dipped a piece of cloth into the water and washed Mrs. Lauritzen's face. Gently he cooled her cheeks and forehead and wiped her hands. I listened to her breathing. Something was very wrong with her.

Breath after breath came in rapid succession, then all breathing stopped for a terribly long time till finally a new cycle began. Even shallower, even faster. And the pauses grew longer and longer. I saw her face in the flickering light of the fire, white and strained with the eyes wide open.

Mr. Lauritzen hovered over her, his face as pale and strained as hers, and tugged at the blanket and rearranged the pillow. He held her shoulders when endless dry coughing interrupted her gasps for air and shook her body. His hands fluttered restlessly and stopped only when her breathing stopped, suspended in mid-action till she breathed again.

No word was spoken, no cry uttered, nothing to disturb the sleepers but the coughing they were used to. I could distinguish Rudi and Frau Hasselmann nestled under their blankets. I heard the fat woman smack her lips and saw her gleaming white pillow. Frau Warnke snored softly. The car was less crowded than the night before. Rabbit coat and the captain were among those sleeping near the fires.

If Mrs. Lauritzen could find some rest, if her breathing returned to some degree of normality, I could rejoin the fire. Right now, there was no escape. Mr. Lauritzen gripped my shoulders in each tense interval between her gasps for air. I knew he was not aware of it; he needed something more to hold than the cold steel of the wheelchair. So we both waited.

And as the night drew on, I fell asleep.

His hand on my shoulder woke me up. Hard as a clamp, with fingers digging into the flesh. It hurt. Yet I could not shake him off—he took no notice of me.

It was quiet and then the wheelchair began to rattle. It rattled like an alarm clock, panicky, penetrating into the odd hours of the night. Our hands flew out to keep it still, to halt the noise. Mrs. Lauritzen's frail body shook, and so did the whole chair. She was thrown back and forth with fury, desperate for air. And her eyes begged us to help.

Then she collapsed. The chair stopped rattling. Her breathing started again, and Mr. Lauritzen stroked her forehead and caressed her cheeks and bent over and whispered long into her ear.

I held one of her hands, bony and cold, and tried to warm it between mine and felt tremors running through her. I breathed in and out consciously and thought to force my rhythm onto her. Yet it seemed to me that each of her breaths was a little weaker, flatter, less substantial than the one before and the pauses between them longer and longer.

"Shouldn't we call for a doctor? Shouldn't we ask for help?"

"It's no use," said Mr. Lauritzen. "A doctor can't help her now."

Then I remembered that doctors were not allowed to leave the Russian zone. They were too scarce. Most of them had fled before the Russians came; the rest were badly needed to treat the strange diseases like typhoid and paratyphoid with all sorts of complications that arose because of the starvation. There would be no doctor aboard the transport.

Mrs. Lauritzen's eyes were clear and she looked directly at the old man and not somewhere into the distance as she had done all the time. Her mouth moved as if she wanted to say something. Mr. Lauritzen put his ear close, listened, and said, "I promise, I promise" several times. I wondered what he had promised.

When he straightened again, she closed her eyes and looked very content and peaceful. Strain and anguish were wiped off her face. For a moment I thought that if she could rest now, tomorrow she would feel a lot better. I did not want to understand why tears were streaming down old Mr. Lauritzen's cheeks. He did not pay any attention to them and let them fall unrestrained. He went on stroking her head.

I held her hand between my hands. It lay absolutely quiet and motionless and was as cold as before. I listened to her breathing and it came slow and feeble, the interval endless between each breath. I thought she was falling asleep and felt drowsy myself. It must have been almost morning and only the fire in front of our car burned; the others had gone out.

Then her hand fluttered briefly in mine. I waited for another move, another sound. I waited and waited, but it never came.

She was dead.

I knew she was dead, though her face had not changed. It looked no different from moments before. Not yet, anyway. Peaceful and content and nevertheless somehow vacant. I let go of her hand; I could not warm it.

I watched Mr. Lauritzen wash her, rearrange her clothing, draw up the blanket, and wrap her up securely. He had stopped weeping and worked purposefully, putting everything back in order. He worked without a sound and frequently glanced around to make sure that nobody observed him. But there were no witnesses but me. The people with us slept soundly; nothing had disturbed their night.

At last Mrs. Lauritzen's appearance seemed to satisfy him; he settled down beside the wheelchair. "Get some rest," he whispered to me. "We have to be alert tomorrow." And soon I heard him breathe regularly. He was asleep.

How could he sleep? Wasn't he going to do anything? Wasn't he going to bury her? Or wake the others and tell them that she had died? If they discovered her death in the morning, they would shove her right off the train, and him with her.

"How do we know it's not contagious!" I could hear rabbit coat scream.

"Fool of an old man, he is dangerous for us all."

"Imagine! Hiding a corpse on the transport! All the way to Cologne."

And no protests would help him, no assurance that he knew the cause of death: old age—or a normally harmless disease, a cough. *Harmless?*

It had killed her. They were not going to be convinced by him. He would be left in the middle of the plain to dig her grave. And then walk back to the district capital.

How could he sleep? Maybe he was old, frail, and exhausted and had cared for her day and night on the transport and who knew how many days and nights before. Maybe he had simply been too weary to fight off sleep any longer. He had held out as long as he could, but now his strength was sapped.

I wondered what he had promised Mrs. Lauritzen and if he still expected me to help him. At least I could try to make sure that nobody found out about Mrs. Lauritzen's death till we reached the next town. Make sure that he was not left alone on the plain. I worried about what would happen when people woke up.

8

I SHOULD HAVE KNOWN
that nobody would pay any special attention to the
motionless form under the blanket. The Lauritzens
had kept to themselves in their windy corner and
had been quiet, except for Mrs. Lauritzen's dry coughs.
Now the old man coughed instead and nobody noticed
the difference.

People were preoccupied with their own needs.
They freshened up, went for water, brewed tea, envied
one another bits of food. The fat woman peeled another hard-boiled egg and swallowed it whole while
every person in the car watched it glide down and
momentarily bulge her throat.

"Let me try that! Eating them whole," cried the
captain and laughed nastily. That was the last egg
they would tolerate watching her eat. You could read
it in their faces: if she dared to eat in front of them
again, they would tear the food out of her hands.

Again we waited.

Only the kids came close enough to worry about.
There was a tense moment with Rudi when he must
have noticed something out of place, strange, without
knowing immediately what it was: he stared and
stared at the wheelchair. When I looked over my

shoulder, I saw that Mr. Lauritzen had balanced his pot of tea on Mrs. Lauritzen's shoulder while he combed his hair and the pot sat completely motionless. I burned my hand when I snatched it off.

Mr. Lauritzen acted as if nothing unusual had happened. He fluffed the pillow, smoothed the blanket, retied the shawl. He talked softly to Mrs. Lauritzen and seemed to listen to her answers. He even went so far as to hold the tea to her lips. And when Frau Warnke asked how his wife was doing, he replied politely and as a matter of course that under the circumstances she was doing very well, very well indeed. But his eyes were reddish, his shoulders less erect, and his coughing persisted. It sounded quite as bad as hers.

"It's only twelve miles to Sandhagen," I said. "It's the first station we reach and they promised us we will move on this morning."

"I am not interested in Sandhagen," he said. "I wonder if I can rebuild the store. How badly was it burned?"

"But . . ." I said and could not go on with all the people listening. Wasn't he getting off, or was he waiting for a larger town?

We had hardly finished the morning chores when the engine arrived. Cheers greeted her. She whistled back, slammed into the transport, sent us rocking, and was immediately connected and proceeded to pull us off the plain. There were no explanations or apologies. After thirty-six hours we traveled on.

We left the heather, the wrecked cottage, the precious pump—my pump. Heaps of ashes from the fires, beds of grass, and piles of wood. The sky turned gray and a harsher wind whipped into the cars. I pulled my jacket tight around me and dug my hands deep into my pockets. It was too cold to sit and swing my legs. And my slight breakfast did not warm me inside. I was hungry.

We passed through more woods and sandy fields. We rattled through the tiny station of Sandhagen, where every clerk lined the platform and watched us with curiosity. We waved to them.

"Congratulations!" they shouted. "We didn't think you'd make it."

We continued to roll speedily for an hour and slowed again as we approached the outskirts of a larger town. First a belt of garden plots, each with its own tiny shed that now housed bombed-out families and refugees. Then factories took over. Every single building had been bombed and burned and blown to pieces, the windows smashed, walls and roof collapsing and black with fire.

The transport headed into a freight station and braked to a halt.

"Another delay," moaned the fat woman and lifted her head from her white pillow.

"Don't let the engine leave us," shrieked Frau Hasselmann, but what did she expect us to do? Throw ourselves in its path?

The captain swore and hobbled to the door. Word traveled along the train that the track ahead was blocked. It would take at least an hour to clear it. We watched the engineer lower himself, inspect his machinery, and calmly march off.

"The bastard, he is going to bolt," muttered the

captain. "If I only could lay my hands on him." He had no chance—we were the seventh car down the line. Why couldn't we have stopped at the main station, where the counter might have offered some thin soup or at least an artificial hot drink? I felt weak with hunger.

Quickly I decided to scout the neighborhood for something to eat. There was at least an hour's wait ahead and I could explore the nearest streets and maybe find a store or people to beg from.

"Shall I help you out?" I asked Mr. Lauritzen and pointed with my head to the wheelchair. He shook his head. He probably thought it easier to get off at the main station.

"Well, I am going to look around." I jumped down from the car and ran the length of the train and out through the back of the station. The cold blast of wind almost turned me back. A path wound through mountains of rubble. Bricks and beams and mortar were piled high; sometimes parts of walls were standing, buried in the debris of the floors above. It was hard to imagine that this had been a street with apartment houses on both sides, with proper little front gardens and curtained windows. Smoke curled from holes where people still lived in caves and cellars or perhaps the first floor of a ruined building. The path widened and led around a blackened wall. Not far away I saw a queue and ran toward it. What were they waiting for?

Why had people queued up? What if they waited for shoe repair? The arrival of imitation leather heels? Important too, but not for me right now. Father had once come home, after hours in line, with some powder to bleach your hair blond. That was after the defeat and the Nazis were gone; nobody cared anymore for blond Germans. But father was almost bald anyway. Another time I had queued up thinking it was a bread line. It moved slowly and people were admitted one at a time. Finally I was ushered into a room to view and perhaps mourn a dead Russian soldier, laid out on a desk and covered with his flag. Tiny blond hairs sprouted on his chin and they had forgotten to close one eye. It seemed to examine each mourner. The blood had seeped through the flag somewhere below his neck and dried in a darker red. I had wondered why people did not reappear with their loaves of bread and I found them all assembled in the rear, guarded by soldiers with rifles. Nobody spoke a word and at last we were marched to the park to bury the soldier. It had been a simple funeral with a few shots and not much weeping.

I looked for a store sign. There was none, but a few words scribbled in chalk on the door said something about the distribution of potatoes. So it was a grocery store!

"Excuse me," I said to the woman ahead of me. "Are they giving out potatoes?"

"Potatoes? I thought they were finally going to let us have the six ounces of fat on number C of our ration cards!" She turned to her neighbor. "Isn't that right? Do you know anything about potatoes, Frau Schmidlin?"

"Potatoes were sold out yesterday," answered Frau Schmidlin. "I am just standing here because I saw the line. I never give up hope." She laughed.

"Neither do I," said the other woman. "One can't afford it these days." But she didn't look very hopeful.

The line crawled slowly and funneled into the door. The exit must be on the other side of a heap of bricks. I inched along and had a sinking feeling in my stomach that I was waiting in vain. It would be more than a miracle if they sold anything to anyone without registration and a regular ration card. I could only think of sauerkraut, salt, baking powder, vinegar, and elderberry tea—which makes me throw up—and even these items the shopkeeper usually reserved for his old customers. I pressed my thumbs for good luck and wished for sauerkraut. It does fill you up. And if the store had received a barrelful, they might be less stingy.

Time passed and I worried too about losing my bag and missing the transport. More about losing the bag. How could I get another sweater or underwear or a dress? I had been stupid not to hide the bag beside the tracks.

What about my container? Or the bottle? Everything was hard to replace.

The line dragged on and I waited uneasily. Then I smelled it: the delicious fishy sour smell of herring salad, the cool mixture of beets, potatoes, onions, cucumbers, and pickled sour herring in mayonnaise. How had they managed to get it? How come they were selling it here in a regular store and not on the black market?

I swallowed the spit that filled my mouth and felt incredibly lucky. I had picked the right store at the right time.

Sure, there was going to be a problem. They had to sell it on ration cards. It had to be a substitute for meat, sugar, bread, or fat. If I did not work it right, I would miss my chance to taste it. So I decided to plead with them that I was starving—which wasn't far from the truth—that I was alone, trying to locate an aunt. I planned to weep and to let my tears run down my cheeks, and the sight of the herring salad would surely bring tears to my eyes. I sobbed to check for the right sound.

"Getting a cold?" inquired the woman ahead. "There's an awful lot of disease around. Did you hear about the Beckers' boy, Frau Schmidlin?"

I did not have to plead or weep. A middle-aged couple behind the counter wordlessly spooned equal shares of herring salad onto brown paper, wrapped them in newspaper, and handed one package to each customer.

"Fifty pfennigs," they said and it made no difference to them if you claimed three members in your family or six and a starving uncle. They handed you one package without demanding food stamps or your name and address. I marveled at mine and hurried out into the road.

Then I smelled my package, tore the newspaper apart, and slurped the salad off the paper with tongue and fingers. I gulped it down like a pig. I did not taste the herring or the beets or the potatoes. I did not crunch the cucumbers or bite the onions. I had no idea what the mayonnaise consisted of: flour, vinegar, and water, or thinned mashed potatoes. I licked the paper clean, dropped it, and ran.

9

HOW MORTIFIED I WAS
when Mr. Lauritzen handed me a potful of soup and a
piece of bread. He had cared enough for me to insist
on an extra ration when some officials unexpectedly
distributed food and I had not been there to demand
my share. He had saved my part even though he could
have easily eaten two shares of soup. And I had given
him no thought and had devoured my herring salad
all by myself. How greedy I had been! What a pig!
I must have blushed, and now I ate the soup carefully.

With the arrival of food, the mood in the wagon had
changed. People were talking, analyzing the soup,
joking about it in mock complaint.

"Not enough salt," stated the fat woman and
reached for her salt shaker.

"Why can it never be really hot?" asked the captain.
"All through the war they expected us to fight on a
cold stomach."

"I wonder if it's horse, dog, or rat," said Rudi.

"Rats have smaller bones," explained Frau Hasselmann and held up a bone thick as a finger. "This
one never belonged to a rat."

"I am so sick of cabbage and beets," they said. "Why

don't they serve roast pork for once?" And their voices were cheerful. Somehow we had been put back on the right track. This freight station would not be our final stop. There would be more meals; the transport would continue. We were not forgotten.

Frau Warnke asked again how Mrs. Lauritzen was doing, and the old man answered that she was not hungry and that they were both looking forward to reaching Cologne before the day was over.

"If there is anything I can do, please let me know," said Frau Warnke.

"Get your kids off my bags," said the captain, who had been listening. "That would be enough help for the moment."

It startled me to hear Mr. Lauritzen talk about reaching Cologne with such certainty and I almost choked on my soup. I had assumed he would get off with Mrs. Lauritzen at the main station. So he planned to carry on with the deception and travel with a dead person! Though I had to admit that it was hard to tell she was dead. She seemed asleep under her cover.

"Why are you doing that?" I whispered. "It's dangerous! People will be furious if they find out. And what are you going to do at the border? They will put you in jail or send you to Siberia! You will never get away with it!"

"I promised Mrs. Lauritzen to bury her in Cologne," said the old man. "That's why we left the district capital. She knew she was going to die soon and she wanted to die at home. Now the least thing I can do for her is to fulfill her last wish. All our family is buried at Central Cemetery—our only daughter too—

70

and she wanted to be close to them. You and I together should be able to let her rest in peace at the very spot she longed for. You promised to help," he added.

I didn't have the heart to point out I had only promised to lift the wheelchair back into the car. *He* had promised to get her back to Cologne and to Central Cemetery and their daughter's grave. I thought I would never care what place I was going to be buried in, though I was not quite sure I wanted to be buried. I rather liked the idea of floating in the ocean or along a slow and muddy river or disintegrating in a pond. I did not want to end up bombed and suffocating in a bunker, and to be lowered into a hole in the earth seemed too similar a fate.

Anyway, I would not ask for promises, dead or alive, and I expected no one to keep them. If I had taken seriously every promise that I had given so far, I would be long dead, killed by the ideas I had promised to fight for with my life.

People ask you to promise this and that. First they invent ceremonies that make your flesh creep, and when you have goose pimples all over and are in no condition to shout "No" or "Never" or walk off or simply laugh, they make you swear.

I had sworn loyalty to Adolf Hitler—loyalty beyond the grave—and after a year or so he was dead, though there were constant rumors that he was not dead at all but living in Argentina. Anyway, the oath must still be valid, and it should bother me that I did not feel especially loyal. But it didn't.

Later I had pledged something to the bishop and they made me kiss his ring. I did not touch it with my mouth, but I repeated their words, so I guess it was a correct promise too. Only I forgot completely what it was about.

Last year I solemnly gave my word to follow Lenin and be a true Pioneer, and for a moment they actually made me believe in it. They played music and we sang and marched and carried flags and the music really got to me.

Now I felt sort of strange. To whom would I have to dedicate my life next? The British, Americans, and French must make you pledge yourself to something.

"I gave her my word last night I would do everything in my power to bury her in Cologne," Mr. Lauritzen was saying. "How can I break it without even trying? How could I sleep? How could I dare to think of her! And how could I *not* think of her? We have been married almost forty-five years!" He looked at me earnestly, his jaws set firmly. Then his face broke and he coughed painfully and the cough left him breathless and trembling for a long time. He was too frail to accomplish his work. He would never make it alone. And he couldn't very well ask any of the other people.

Actually, I would not have minded at all trying to deceive the captain and Frau Hasselmann, the fat woman, the mousy man, rabbit coat, and the rest. I could imagine how furious they would be if they ever found out. I would not mind trying to fool the authorities at the border—I was already traveling with false papers. Even if the fat woman had asked me to help and smuggle one of her boxes across, I wouldn't have turned her down.

It was a challenge and I liked it. I was free to take

it up. Even in Cologne I had plenty of time to help bury Mrs. Lauritzen. We were forty hours behind schedule and the people from the school must have given up their watch for me by now. No reason to keep out of sight there. I was free to do what I wanted and stay as long as I liked.

Not that there was any obligation. Even if I took it seriously, I had promised nothing more than to help Mr. Lauritzen once or twice with the wheelchair, whereas he had committed himself to bury his wife in Cologne.

So I decided to help him for the fun of it.

"Attention, attention!" they shouted along the train, and the wheels shrieked. The fat woman settled back into her pillow, Frau Hasselmann called Rudi away from the door, the mousy man adjusted his glasses, and the Warnke kids licked the last traces of soup from their pots.

"We will be in Cologne tonight," sighed rabbit coat, but she wouldn't bet on it when the captain offered her his money.

We rolled out of the freight station past more bombed areas and braked again as we entered the main station. Every platform there was packed with people and luggage. Bad times do not keep people home; on the contrary, they encourage people to travel more than ever. If the mail does not work and the telephone is out of order and the newspapers do not print news, you have to see for yourself what's going on elsewhere. And tickets are really no problem; you can barter for them with the right payment.

Some people traveled because railroad stations were the only places to look for information if you were searching for your family. And how many had lost theirs in the tumultuous days of the war! Every available wall was plastered with messages: *Who has seen Kurt Schroeder, last stationed near Moscow? Hermann Reissenbaum wrote from Italy, April '43.*

Like my brother Jochen, soldiers were missing all over Europe. Wolfgang and I had glued messages on the wall at the district capital and at our station asking people to contact us if they knew anything about Jochen. We didn't know how to describe him; he must have changed during the two years he had been gone and there were many with only one leg. So we wrote nothing but his name and the name of his hospital. We liked to pore over the lists, always hoping to discover one person we had seen somewhere before. One single match!

There were endless lists of lost children: *Inge Bobzin, blond, blue-eyed, disappeared between Kolberg and Stettin, three-and-one-half years old, nickname Sissy.*

Messages for displaced families: *Karl, we moved in with Aunt Emma in Bamberg.*

Walls and walls full of notes and I carried some of mine along to post everywhere, once I had my own address. So there was reason enough to travel just to study the walls. Or to see and visit your family.

Other travelers were black marketeers. And I regretted not being old or tough enough to be one of them. They traveled in style—like the fat woman. They had all the necessary papers, the right coupons and food stamps for every area, picnic lunches, the knowledge of trains and schedules, the right commodities to bribe any official at critical times.

How did they get them? They were dealers, clever, hard-nosed, and bold. Black markets were everywhere. All kinds of things were bought, sold, and traded. Textiles from the south, fish from the sea, molasses, butter, eggs, bacon, and potatoes from the farms, jewelry, rugs, and paintings from the rich, leather from the shoemaker's supplies, building material from the city inspectors, and everything that the occupying armies had to offer or that could be stolen from them: nylons, coffee, alcohol, canned goods, cigarettes. And the American cigarette served as the new standard currency. Everything was worth so many American cigarettes. That made the Americans richer than anybody, since they controlled them.

There were big successful black marketeers and unimportant ones.

Father had been a lousy black marketeer. With a couple of silver spoons, he walked from farm to farm and returned with a single egg. He had not even tried to talk the farmer into a better deal.

Mother—shivering with excitement—traded a brooch—grandmother's heirloom—at the corner of Steinstrasse and Roter Platz with an equally inexperienced black marketeer and came home with some eighteenth-century poetry, a book she had always wanted and could have bought probably at the local bookstore.

Wolfgang secretly carried our silver teapot to the same place and limped home with a bump as big as an egg on his head and a bruise on his leg. Someone had knocked him over, grabbed the pot, and run. Later he traded his collection of Hitler stamps with a Russian officer and got fifty pounds of potatoes, a bottle of vodka, and a ride on a tank. I tried to trade mine, but was only offered the potatoes and the vodka, so I kept them. Father literally threw them away for a pair of slippers.

Kruegers, who owned two houses across the street, always had more than they could eat and bought houses and land everywhere. It was said they fleeced old ladies of their jewels for some measly food and made fantastic deals on the black market in Berlin. Luesewitz had filled his farm with the most beautiful Persian rugs till the officials found his milk cow hidden in a secret compartment—his price for butter had been outrageous—and they gave him three years of hard labor for cheating people and sabotaging the economy.

So the station was full of different travelers. Fortunately we rolled steadily past the mobbed platform and did not give them a chance to squeeze in with us or throw us off. Soon we left the station and city behind.

 **10**

IT STARTED TO RAIN. FAT lazy drops fell and the wind pushed them into my face. I closed the door partly to protect me and Mrs. Lauritzen from getting drenched. The old man had taken refuge from a very bad draft behind the wheelchair and coughed. I shivered, regarded her blanket with longing, and thought that she could not get much colder and really did not need it. Mr. Lauritzen could use it much better right now. But I didn't dare pull it off her. How could I?

For hours the land was flat and uninteresting. Field after soggy field untended under a gray sky. Villages squatted among them, treeless, naked, brown. People inside the wagon dozed and huddled under blankets and few talked. Frau Hasselmann snored and Rudi cautiously crept over to join me at the door and we played "animal, vegetable, and mineral" with Mr. Lauritzen; no one was allowed to think of anything edible. Rudi broke the rule once, letting us guess "Easter egg hunt" and Mr. Lauritzen broke the rule twice with "frankfurter," the hot dog and a person from the town of Frankfurt, and "Napoleon," the French emperor and a brandy that Rudi and I had never even heard about. So we had to exclude double meanings too.

Then the land rose, climbed over hills, overflowed into gentle valleys. Woods appeared as dark blotches in the brown: oaks, beeches, firs. The rain stopped and the soft gray mass of sky separated into lumpy clouds.

The land rose higher, the valleys dipped deeper, pines and firs covered their flanks. Streams crossed the valleys. Villages were tucked into the folds of the woods. Groaning, the train crawled along. It had lost all speed and wheezed uphill. For hours we had sat without moving. My feet itched. I wanted to jump out and run along with the train.

It had been one of the feats of the big kids back

home years ago, when the track to Langenan was still in use. They made wild bets on where and when to jump off and leap back on again, while the younger kids watched out for the conductor or interfering adults and cheered them on. Grownups warned with gory details of chopped-off arms and legs and headless bodies, but nothing ever happened. But the train was discontinued due to a lack of spare parts and the big kids were drafted into the army, sent to the front to fight, and most of them did not come back. So I had never had a chance to try my courage.

It looked promising here. The embankment was level and the slope stretched for another mile or two into a soft open meadow. But the running board, set rather high, would make it a bit difficult to get back on the train. Not impossible though.

"Let's jump out and run along the track," I said to Rudi. "Aren't you tired of sitting and sitting? My legs are killing me!"

"My *mother* will kill me! Never mind my legs." Rudi looked over to her and she was still snoring. "Do you think the others would wake her up?"

"Sure," I said. The fat woman, the captain, Frau Warnke, rabbit coat—all of them would waken her immediately. No doubt about that.

"I'll do it anyway," announced Rudi.

So we leaped, landed on our feet, and skipped along the meadow faster than the transport. It screamed and shouted behind us.

"Will you get back this very minute!" shrieked Frau Hasselmann. Rudi hesitated a split second, straightened his shoulders, and ran on.

"It's fun!" he cried.

"Get back at once!" shrieked Frau Hasselmann. I looked over my shoulder to see how mad she was and stumbled over a rock and fell flat on my face.

"Damn brat! I hope she broke her leg," cried the captain, as my car passed me.

"She'll miss the transport!"

"Serves her right!"

"Rudi, get back here," shrieked Frau Hasselmann, "right now!" I didn't have to see her face to know how furious she was. I guess I would have obeyed her too, just as Rudi did. I saw him falter and search for me; then he ran, leaped, and was grabbed by many hands and pulled inside. And I am sure his mother slapped him.

I picked myself off the grass, and people watched me curiously out of each open door as the transport rolled past. If I didn't want to miss it completely, I would need some luck. Wasn't the slope less steep? Didn't the wheels turn faster? The train groan less? I ran and passed the last three cars.

"What's your hurry?" they laughed.

"Are you trying to catch a rabbit?"

I dashed along and beat the next three cars.

"Competing with Jesse Owens?"

I was level with my own car and the captain barred the entrance with his crutch, as if joking. I ran and waited for him to make room for me—it was urgent, the train was speeding up—and then I saw a black shoe with a dark-blue sock shoot forward and kick against the captain's leg. He needed his crutch to steady himself and I leaped and reached the running

board and pulled myself in. Nobody blocked my way.
"Don't you dare do something like that again!"
they threatened, closing around me, and I felt each
waiting for the other to hit me first as I tried to catch
my breath.

"Think of your poor mother!" sighed the fat woman.
"You gave me such a scare!"

"She doesn't have one," cried Rudi from the corner,
where Frau Hasselmann had banished him, and his
cheek was red with the marks of her hand. This time
he saved me. People are reluctant to hit an orphan.
They pushed me roughly over to Mr. Lauritzen.

"Why don't we give her a few to teach her a lesson?"
asked the mousy man, but it was too late for that now.

I had been thinking of my mother. I knew she
would have kicked up a fuss as much as Frau Hasselmann. But she had allowed me to leave alone, so now
I was responsible for myself and if I felt like doing
something not quite responsible, I was still responsible. Anyway, if people had minded their own business, Rudi and I would have had no trouble.

"I am so sorry to hear about your mother," said
Mr. Lauritzen when I sat down near him. He beamed
friendliness and sympathy. "I should have wondered
about why you traveled all by yourself, but I am afraid
I only cared about my own burden. Are you joining
your father and perhaps a sister or brother in Cologne?"

"Yes," I said curtly, and he must have felt that I
did not want to be questioned further.

He changed the subject: "I used to run in my
younger days. That's how I met Mrs. Lauritzen. She

stood at the finish line. I was not the winner. Actually, I came in last."

I looked down. He wore blue socks and black shoes. "My brother Jochen was a pretty good runner," I said. "He twice won the hundred-meter dash at home. He was wounded in the war. They had to amputate his leg and now he is missing."

"How awful!" Mr. Lauritzen shook his head sadly. "This terrible war."

"I am going to search for him," I said. "Perhaps I can find him."

"I will pray for your success," said the old man simply.

I crouched in my place and watched the mountains and valleys go by. We traveled slowly and must still be far away from Cologne. We had not yet crossed the border and it was almost evening. The sky was clearing and showed pale frosty patches of blue. The wind blew icy. Now we closed the door against the cold and I could only guess the country behind it. The wheels clanked over the tracks, and the transport rattled along wearily. Then we stopped.

"That must be the border," said Mr. Lauritzen, sounding hopeful. "We must be there now."

"The border!" cried the fat woman. "Do you think they will search each one of us?" And she rummaged excitedly in her handbag. Was she going to swallow her diamonds?

"My papers are correct," stated the mousy man as if there had been any doubt. "I had them checked and rechecked."

"There is no such thing as correct papers," said

Frau Hasselmann. "It all depends on who does the checking."

But it was not the border.

We stood in a tiny railroad station, brightly lit and full of German officials. Each one in uniform. Here was organization!

Before anyone of us could ask what was going to happen, they marched up to each car and announced that food was being prepared, water was available in the main building, restrooms had been set up to the left—rather primitive restrooms, they added apologetically—and we would drive on in less than an hour.

"There is still some of the old spirit," commented the captain, his voice full of pride. "Makes you feel better right away."

"Why can't it be like this everywhere?" Rabbit coat puffed herself up.

Like this? For heaven's sake why?

Commands were shouted and people of the first two cars were marched over to the left. More commands and everyone who could walk in the following two cars was led to the main building. The occupants of all other cars had to wait for their orderly return. When I jumped on the platform I was harshly told to get back into place or they would make sure I would go hungry.

"What do you think you are doing!" one of them cried. "Didn't you hear us? There has to be *order*. What will happen if everyone does what he chooses to do?"

I thought—but I took care and did not say it out loud—that people would go to the restrooms and fetch water, just as they were now ordered to do, only they would go at their own speed and would decide themselves where to go first—the restrooms or the water—or perhaps they would even prefer to stroll up and down the platform after hours of immobility. I myself felt like racing the length of the transport, having a drink at the faucet, paying a visit to the restrooms, and then washing up at the faucet. In that order. And I could see no harm in it.

Instead I and Mr. Lauritzen and everyone else waited for ten minutes in our car, for fifteen minutes in line at the restrooms, for twenty minutes at the faucet, and for another fifteen minutes inside our car before dinner arrived.

"I am still thirsty," wailed one of the Warnke kids. "Can't I go and have another drink?"

"Water or soup! Take your choice," said the captain. "You heard them as well as everyone else."

"But it's so stupid," cried Rudi. "There is nobody at the faucet now!" Frau Hasselmann boxed him behind the ears.

A kettle with soup and baskets of bread were wheeled along the platform. More orders were shouted. They made us line up inside the boxcar—which was really ridiculous with all the people and luggage— and step forward one at a time to receive a ladle full of soup and a hunk of bread. I resolutely pushed the wheelchair to the door while Mr. Lauritzen tried to hold me back.

"If they ask her to speak up for herself," he whispered, "what can we do?"

"What will people think if you don't demand her

share?" I hissed back and let him pass ahead. His voice trembled when he requested his portion and hers, but it was hardly noticeable and nobody became suspicious.

The soup was not bad: lukewarm water, a few beets, cabbage leaves, and two or three tiny cubes of potatoes—if you were lucky. Enough to kill the Warnke kid's thirst. At least he never said another word about it. Mr. Lauritzen went through the motion of helping his wife with her food and he smacked his lips for her, secretly spooning her share into my container. But we saved her hunk of bread for breakfast.

Nobody else got a second portion. They carried the soup and bread away from the transport and when the captain offered—half-kidding and half-serious—to take care of the leftovers for them, they did not bother to answer.

"They must raise pigs," said the fat woman, "just as Dornberg did, who administered the Displaced Persons camp in Tretow before they jailed him for whatever he was supposed to have done in Poland during the war, when his name was Mueller. Or Schulz. I don't remember which. Anyway, he raised the pigs in abandoned bunkers. His organization was nearly perfect. You couldn't hear a squeak through those walls."

"It's very much against regulations to raise pigs in poorly ventilated areas," said the mousy man seriously and cringed when the captain roared with laughter.

Officials ordered the doors closed and the people obeyed because they assumed the transport would continue and because they always obeyed. We sat and waited in the dark while they marched up and down the platform.

Mr. Lauritzen coughed for a long time. I knew he must be worried. He had so firmly believed that we would arrive in Cologne by evening and now we had not even crossed the border and were stuck in a little station where people would not be at all inclined to help him with Mrs. Lauritzen. Quite to the contrary. She had started to look a little strange. One could see it each time the blanket slipped off her face. She looked grim now, and Mr. Lauritzen had said it was rigor mortis and he hoped it would last a long time because as long as rigor mortis persisted nothing else would happen to her—like falling apart. And I didn't care to remember about the people I had helped dig out of cellars.

But rigor mortis or no rigor mortis, people were going to notice soon that she did not move and never said a word, that she neither ate nor drank, and that he coughed instead of her. If we didn't reach Cologne by morning, we would be in a real mess. I wondered what the penalties were for transporting a dead person. Would they send me home? Or to a camp? Or to Siberia? And would they ever tell Mr. Lauritzen what they did with Mrs. Lauritzen while they kept him in jail? At home they buried Arno Schwarz—he had died of typhoid in my house—while his mother was still too sick to go to the cemetery and later nobody knew where his grave was. She wandered among the graves till they carried her out on a stretcher.

I woke up when the train rattled to a start and had no idea what time it was. I felt stiff and cold and cramped and went back to sleep as fast as I could. When I woke up again, the transport was grinding to a halt.

"Where are we? Open the door! Quick! Open the door!" commanded voices from all sides. I struggled with the door and blinked into the bright morning light: another empty platform, a rusty second track, a building with its dirty brown antibombing paint. Immediately a loudspeaker boomed down on us.

II

"EVERY PERSON MUST leave the train. This transport ends here. Every person must leave the train. This transport ends here!"

We looked at one another and smiled. We had made it. We had crossed the border during the night. Nobody had checked us and now we had arrived in Cologne. However, I was a bit puzzled, since mother and father had told me Cologne was a large town with the gigantic cathedral right across from the station on the banks of the river Rhine.

This station did not seem like much; it had not even been considered worth bombing. And nowhere could I discover a cathedral or a river. My view was blocked by a lumberyard and a gas storage tank. But perhaps I was facing the wrong direction, and anyway mother and father had never seen Cologne themselves.

"I can't tell you how happy I am." The old man glowed rosily and worked around the wheelchair, tugging the blanket tighter and pulling it high to conceal Mrs. Lauritzen's face.

"But where are we?" cried Frau Hasselmann. "I don't recognize anything!"

"You mean to say it is not Cologne?" asked the fat woman, who bent forward so that I could see into the bag on her lap right into a nest of eggs.

"Nonsense," exclaimed both rabbit coat and the mousy man. "You must be wrong. It's just not possible."

"Some suburb! They all look alike." The captain glanced up and down the platform. "I have never . . ." The loudspeaker drowned his words and repeated its message.

"But look at the sign! Look at the sign!" Rudi pointed excitedly to the far end of the platform. "It says Eisenach. That isn't near Cologne!"

And while everybody leaned out of the carriage to see the sign, the loudspeaker went on impersonally: "The border is closed temporarily. Nobody will be cleared through the checkpoints today. Every person must leave the train now. This transport ends here. A school has been prepared to accommodate all of you. Proceed at once to the Ernst Thälmann Elementary School. Proceed at once to the school."

I had listened with growing excitement. Then I took my bag and jumped off. I forgot about the Lauritzens. There was going to be turmoil and I wanted to come out ahead. I only thought of being the first person from the transport to reach the school, of claiming the best classroom, the softest bed, the most blankets for myself. I only thought of exploring our new shelter, of investigating the kitchen, the dining halls, of being the first in line at the food counter.

So I did not join in the general uproar and protest. People shouted for the stationmaster, the Russian commandant. They abused all officials, with special reference to the lying clerks back home who had never hinted at the possibility of anything but a smooth journey. They cursed the whole state of affairs and their own powerlessness and threatened to pay them all back once they had a chance. And their chance would come; those in power would not wield it long.

The loudspeaker repeated its message mechanically.

Suddenly it was quiet. Russian soldiers appeared. They marched up the stairs and spread out along the platform in a single row from one end of the transport to the other. They held rifles in their hands and watched us with empty faces. Their officer fired a few shots into the station building and two windows splintered and the glass shattered on the ground.

Now people became busy. They poured out of the wagons and piled their baggage on the platform. They collected their families and groups, loaded boxes, bags, bedrolls, suitcases, and babies. They shuffled along the platform and huddled together, taking care to avoid contact with the soldiers. Keeping their heads averted and grumbling, they trekked down the stair-case of the underpass, up the opposite stairs, and out through the station building. Glass crunched under their feet.

I wiggled in and around the people and hustled

along the platform. I had passed through the tunnel and was climbing up the stairs when I remembered Mr. Lauritzen. Immediately a lot of excuses flashed through my mind: the transport had ended, so he did not need my help to go to the nearest official and tell him about his wife's death; there was nothing I could do; I would only confuse things since we were not even related; there was no likelihood of reaching Cologne now; it didn't make sense to try any longer, not with a closed border and all of us confined in a strange school for who knew how long.

Nevertheless my steps slowed down and finally the crowd carried me along and dumped me at the top of the stairs. I stood wavering. At least I should have said good-by.

"Come on," cried Rudi. "I'm glad you ditched the old guy and his wheelchair. Come on, we'll have some fun at the school!"

"Where is the old couple?" asked Frau Warnke. "Are they not coming to the school?"

Frau Hasselmann pulled Rudi with her, and Frau Warnke and the kids disappeared through the door. The fat woman wheezed past, overloaded with her belongings.

"You could lend me a hand," she said. "I'll pay you —better than the old man."

I shook my head and turned back. I was ashamed. Rudi was right. I had ditched Mr. and Mrs. Lauritzen and for nothing more than a better place in the food line and a blanket. Here I was thinking only of myself. Hadn't I blamed mother and father for making things simple for themselves by getting rid of me, and wasn't

I doing the same now by deserting the old man? There was no reason yet to give up the goal of bringing Mrs. Lauritzen to Cologne and fulfilling her last wish. It was only going to be tougher, but didn't I like that challenge? At least we could try.

Mr. Lauritzen was the only person left in the car—he and the wheelchair. Although many others were milling about on the platform, nobody had offered to help him, just as I had run away without bothering about him. He stood looking forlorn in the open door, evidently trying to figure out how to lower the heavy chair three feet down onto the platform by himself. His face brightened when he saw me.

"I was afraid Frau Hasselmann had taken you with her." He smiled.

"She tried, but I escaped." I do not blush when I lie.

"I am a little discouraged." He sighed. "I was counting on waking up in Cologne."

"We'll get there," I said firmly. "I promise. We will get there." And I intended to keep my promise—a real promise, freely given. I would do all I could to help him, no matter how difficult the situation. From now on they would have to tear me away from the wheelchair. And I felt good about it.

The first problem was to get it safely on the ground. Mr. Lauritzen rolled it forward and I was supposed to bear its full weight. Twice I cried out that I didn't have the right hold and was going to drop it, and poor Mr. Lauritzen pulled the wheelchair back in at the last second and panted. The third time he did not have the right grip and together we heaved the chair back in. We both must have been stronger two days ago on the plain. The fourth time everything seemed to work all right, but suddenly the old man started to cough and he coughed with such explosive force that he could not help letting go of the chair. I staggered under the weight. I swayed from side to side, desperately trying to keep my balance. Pitching to the left, I already saw in my mind poor Mrs. Lauritzen spill on the hard dirty platform. But just before I collapsed, the burden was miraculously lifted and the wheelchair put gently on the ground. One of the Russian guards had come to the rescue. Now he hoisted Mr. Lauritzen off the boxcar and, his face flushed crimson, warded off our confused thanks.

"Babushka?" he asked and pointed to the lifeless body under the blanket.

We nodded.

"Babushka far." He slapped his chest and waved his arm toward the east and smiled broadly. Then he picked me up, gave me a forceful hug and a kiss on each cheek, and with a face even redder than before, he marched back to his post, picking up his gun off the ground, and stared above us.

I don't know who was more embarrassed. My face felt hot; I must have blushed as much as he. You cannot be hugged and kissed by a Russian soldier. We were enemies; we had fought and killed each other; we still hated each other. Besides, friendly contact between Russians and Germans, called "fraternization" (which just means behaving like brothers), was forbidden for them as well as for us.

And he had hugged and kissed me in front of hundreds of people and his own comrades and officers!

He must have forgotten where he was, and Mrs. Lauritzen probably had reminded him of his own grandmother far away in Russia. I hoped none of his officers had seen us. And I was relieved to know that Rudi and his mother had left before the incident. Rudi would never have let me forget it. Quickly I threw all our bags on Mrs. Lauritzen's lap and pushed the chair forward: I had to get out of this station.

Mr. Lauritzen caught up with me at the staircase. Together we bumped the chair from step to step, and Mrs. Lauritzen's body jumped up and down as if alive and hung over the armrest so he had to straighten her in the tunnel.

Together we pulled the chair up and it was good to know that Mrs. Lauritzen did not feel the weight of the luggage nor the chair bouncing from step to step. It would have given her a terrific headache. In front of the station we breathed deeply and smiled at each other.

"He shouldn't have kissed me," I said. "I could have died!"

"He didn't think about what he was doing," said Mr. Lauritzen. "Wasn't it nice of him to help us?"

"Still, he shouldn't have kissed me."

The rest of the way was easy. We wheeled the chair along the road. Stragglers sat on the curbs—kids guarding belongings, older people resting. They pointed the way to the school, which was not far. Four blocks of suburban streets with none of the houses bombed or burned. Then I saw a wire fence and behind it the familiar cinder-covered yard and red-brick buildings. A gate with the name of the school and through the paint of the new name showed the old one: Horst Wessel Elementary School. Horst Wessel had been a young Hitler storm trooper with lots of places named after him—a square at home and a street in the next town and a song that everyone knew. I could recite his biography by heart. Ernst Thälmann had been a communist labor leader, and since the German defeat his name had been painted on many street signs and houses and squares, but the paint was bad and peeled off easily and people simply needed lots more time to become as familiar with him as they were with Horst Wessel. I hardly knew his biography and it was surprising that the announcer at the station had not stumbled over his name.

"If you wait here, I'll go and look around inside," I said. "It's easier for one person."

"A cool, secluded area," admonished Mr. Lauritzen, "as far away as possible from the people who traveled with us so far!"

Was he serious?

The grounds and buildings were a madhouse, swarming with people. A post in the middle of the yard gave different directions: Red Cross, Delousing Station, Mess Hall, First Aid, Information. I flowed along with the crowd and found Information and it was closed with a note pinned to the door announcing that there was no information. And Red Cross was shut with a note stating that they would return in two weeks. First Aid promised to be open at six o'clock only for people about to die and were sorry to be out of bandages, crutches, and aspirin. The corridors around the Mess Hall reeked of cabbage soup, so at least the kitchen was in operation. I did not try the

Delousing Station, because its odor makes me want to throw up and I didn't want to give them a chance to douse me with their stinking powder. They were known to assume that everyone had lice. They acted first and asked questions later and generally they were right.

It was tedious to get from station to station. The buildings were teeming with people. There must have been other trainloads before us because some groups seemed quite at home in the classrooms. Wash dried on ropes strung from blackboards to windows, and large areas were curtained off for privacy with sheets and blankets. Desks and chairs were used to barricade corners and to separate special territories.

I asked a friendly–looking woman if one could settle anywhere one wanted to.

"Sure," she said, "but you'll be lucky if you can find a square inch. A big crowd arrived just now. Try the cellar!"

"Grandfather can't manage stairs," I explained. "Is nobody here to tell you what to do?"

"In the week I have been here I haven't seen a soul —an official soul," she replied, "but we do get some food regularly."

A whole week! No wonder they were crowded.

I wandered along the corridors and peered into classroom after classroom and found them all fully occupied. I went up the stairs on the first and second floors and they were jammed too. There was no separate empty wing for our transport. We were meant to squeeze right in with the others.

The buildings stank. They stank of unwashed bodies and overused lavatories, of stale cabbage and

sweat, and of ink and dust from former schooldays—
and of delousing powder. Not a single classroom
promised shelter and safety for Mrs. Lauritzen. Each
held too many people too close together. They were
bound to become curious and look under the blanket.
Also they generated too much heat. We needed a room
for ourselves.

A room for ourselves! The classrooms were mobbed;
the gym was bursting with people; halls, corridors,
and staircases were packed. I wandered around looking for a room for ourselves. Somewhere in the cellar
I ran into Rudi, Frau Hasselmann, Frau Warnke and
the kids and was greeted as an old friend. Hadn't we
shared long hours together?

"Isn't this terrible?" sighed Frau Hasselmann. "Have
you heard anything about how long they are going
to keep us here?"

"Why don't you stay with us since you are no longer
helping the old couple," said Frau Warnke. "He did
turn back, didn't he?"

"She left him high and dry inside the train." Rudi
grinned. "I wonder what happened to him and the
wheelchair?"

"As it happens," I explained to him coldly, "I am
right now trying to find room for him and the chair."

"I am sure we could make room for all of you,"
said Frau Warnke, and Frau Hasselmann nodded.

"Old friends should stick together," she said, forgetting that we had not been too friendly during our
journey.

But I thanked them and wandered off. The stairs
into the cellar were too steep.

The captain hailed me in the hall: "Hey you! You

get around, don't you? Have you seen the lady with the many boxes? You know, she is rather . . ." and he blew his cheeks.

I knew he meant the fat woman and I had watched her bargain for a corner of a classroom with some of the contents of her bag. Now I guided him to the room where she rested in what must have been the principal's chair, her head on her white pillow. From the happy noises he made greeting her you would not have guessed that he had limped past her without a backward glance earlier.

"Nice to see you," she said. "Nice to see a familiar face. There should be room enough for you. Make yourself comfortable!" She indicated some boxes.

"You mean I can move in here? With Mr. Lauritzen?" I had not reckoned with that much friendliness.

"Who is talking about you?" said the captain, laughing. "Don't you know it's everyone for himself?" And he stretched out near the fat woman.

I hated them both.

I must have walked by that particular door a number of times, a narrow door open to reveal the janitor's closet and his equipment: brooms, brushes, pails, a ladder, a mountain of boxes. Suddenly it struck me as the only possible place, in fact, the ideal spot—how can one be so blind—and I crashed rudely through the crowd to fetch Mr. Lauritzen. If only nobody discovered my place in the meantime!

12

BUT WE WERE LUCKY. After I cleaned the closet, it was big enough to hold half of the wheelchair. The other half stuck out into the corridor, still shielded on one side by the open door. Mrs. Lauritzen was almost completely protected from view if the old man guarded her only vulnerable side.

"How clever of you!" applauded Mr. Lauritzen. "Mrs. Lauritzen will feel at home. We have a similar closet off to the right of the store. For storing potatoes in the dark to prevent their sprouting. And vinegar."

Pleased with myself, I went off to scout for food, blankets, and news. The Mess Hall was still closed, but the smell of cabbage soup had grown stronger. It had to be ready soon. All the blankets around were already being used.

Listening for news, I mingled with groups of people. The rumors were mixed. Some said we would be shipped back home in the morning, or to Dresden or to Leipzig, depending on where your transport had come from. The border had been permanently sealed. Others said war between the Russians and the Western Allies was imminent; they had observed large troop movements along their route. That was such an old story, bound to be revived every time; a tank rolled somewhere or a regiment marched because people just couldn't accept the idea that the war was over and that they had been defeated. They wanted others to be defeated too.

I also heard there was an outbreak of typhoid and we all would be quarantined right here in the school for the next three weeks. That was the reason we had encountered no officials. They were too scared to be confined with us and only let the kitchen people in through a secret passage. Three weeks was much too late for Mrs. Lauritzen. No rigor mortis lasted that long. I would have to find a way out.

Some people said that they had been waiting for the border to reopen for more than a week and that at least four more transports had arrived in the meantime.

Some people said the food was reasonable and sufficient; others declared it stank. It all depends on what you are used to. Frau Warnke was going to be content with a lot less than the fat woman.

One transport had been turned back, another from Berlin allowed across the supposedly shut border. Nobody knew how the system worked or if there was a system. Information had been closed continuously and the cooks and kitchen help and First Aid people refused to answer questions. Yet the camp must exist on some official list. How else could one account for the announcer at the station, the distribution of food, and the operation of the Delousing Station ten hours a day? (First Aid was on a much more limited basis.) Who directed the camp was a mystery.

In my mind I sorted what I had heard. I discarded

the war rumor as too stale, nor did I believe they would make us walk back—not after herding us into this school. An outbreak of typhoid or another infectious disease seemed more likely; there were enough lice and fleas and dirt and overcrowding to spread them around. But perhaps there was a simple reason: the checkpoint was closed because its commandant felt like it, just as ours had ordered schools, stores, and offices closed for two days and proclaimed a derby on the old race course last summer. Or the guards were celebrating one of their holidays and too drunk to work. Last November we had been out of water for five days while our commandant was toasting the anniversary of the Russian revolution and could not sign his permission to operate the new pump.

Rudi touched my arm. "Sorry," he said. "Where are you now?"

"In a closet," I answered. "Heard anything interesting?"

"There is this guy who talks about illegal ways across. Come on, I'll show you." Rudi steered me into the next building and right into a large group. "That's him!" he whispered.

A man in tattered pieces of former uniforms—an air force coat, an infantry shirt, new boots, definitely not Russian—was talking in a low and somehow secretive voice. "You don't have to wait till the border opens. You don't want to wait that long. It can be three days, three weeks, or three months. You can't afford to wait. There are plenty of ways to get across. It's done all the time. Trust me and my friend. We have the experience."

"And how many get robbed and killed on the way

over!" shouted Rudi and wiggled out of their circle. Suddenly everybody knew of suspicious operations at the border. Criminals were supposed to have organized border gangs, which preyed on innocent travelers. They collected their victims at stations and camps, charged enormous sums, and left them somewhere in the woods more dead than alive. Whole families had disappeared, others escaped only with their lives. It was not safe to trust an unknown guide. Didn't he look dangerous?

I was not so sure and regretted that Rudi had messed up an opportunity to ask more questions. Him and his big mouth. Not every single guide would be a killer. Anyway, we had to take a chance. Mrs. Lauritzen could not wait. We had to get her across the border as soon as possible. So I followed the man around as he approached another group. They were talking about diseases and he brought their conversation cleverly around to what was called "crossing the green border." Only when his listeners seemed truly interested did he disclose himself as a guide.

"I could bring you all across today. This very morning. Or afternoon if you prefer."

"But is it really safe?"

"It's as safe as things are today. I wouldn't suggest you try it on your own!"

"And how much will it cost?"

"One hundred marks for each person, fifty for each piece of luggage, one half paid in advance, the rest on the other side."

Three people signed up; the others hesitated.

"It only takes three hours," he continued to persuade

them, "and there will be a cart for your luggage. Take as much as you like; you won't have to carry a bit! Heaven knows how long they are going to keep the checkpoints closed."

I had enough money for me and the Lauritzens. Though I did not quite trust him, he seemed to know his business and was prepared to lead us across today —without further delays. That was important.

"How about a wheelchair?" I asked. "My grandmother can't walk."

"Out of the question!" He did not bother to consider my problem.

"It's less trouble than a cartful of luggage," I said.

"I told you the answer is *NO*." He shoved me out of his circle.

"Watch out. He is going to rob you!" I shouted angrily. "He is out for your money and belongings and will leave you all dead in the woods."

He would have to start recruiting somewhere else. But he had given me an idea: I only had to find another guide. A kid—one of the local kids who knew the woods just as well as I knew the woods back home. There must be kids who went across the border for fun. Or some who crossed with their knapsacks full of goods for the black market. They wouldn't mind taking a wheelchair with an old woman and perhaps a small cart for Mr. Lauritzen in case he could not hike for three hours.

If only I could find such a kid! I would begin looking after lunch. The odor of cabbage soup was too tempting, reminding me of my empty stomach, and had now permeated all the buildings. So I fetched our containers and lined up. Rudi had managed to conquer a place right at the door, but I was not very far behind.

After a while a window opened and let out a cloud of exquisite-smelling steam. I sucked it in and my stomach twitched wildly. A perspiring face appeared in the mist.

"Line up! On the double! Two in a row!" boomed the voice, and people shuffled into the prescribed order. Which again made no sense, because the narrow corridor was much better suited for single file. Less chance of bumping into one another and spilling soup. But try and tell that to any official! What do they care?

A ladle swung rhythmically and emptied into pot, plate, or can—whatever the person possessed—and a hand pushed a piece of bread forward.

"Next! Next!" growled the voice impatiently. "Haven't got all day."

I presented mine and Mr. Lauritzen's pot.

"Three, please," I said. "We are three. Grandfather, grandmother, and me."

"Have to come themselves! Didn't you hear me?" was the rough reply.

I had heard her.

"But grandmother is in a wheelchair!" I sounded close to tears.

"Bring the chair! It has wheels, hasn't it? I won't be fooled! One portion for everyone and they have to apply in person. The stories they tell me!" she said with a scornful laugh and at the same time dumped a ladleful of soup partly into my pot and partly over my hand, and I could have cried because my hand hurt and half of the precious stuff—boiling hot—was dripping on the floor. Instead I bit my lips, said nothing, took the bread, and left. I was going to come back for more.

Next time I would take my jacket off. I would be a different kid, especially if I kept my mouth shut. I would show her how stupid her rules were. In the dim light and thick steam she could not even see clearly who was right in front of her, let alone recognize the same person two or three hundred people later.

Rudi lined up right after me. Also in disguise: now he wore a cap and a green sweater and pretended to see me for the first time.

"It smells delicious," he said. "I wonder what it tastes like. Where do you come from?" "Dresden," I replied. "We arrived a week ago. And the soup smells better than it tastes."

"You sure made a mess of this place," he said snobbishly. "It's filthy and it stinks! And nothing works. For example this line here: people could come and ask for another portion five times in a row."

But they could not, because they ran out of soup even before I received a third share. So we each had only one portion, Mr. Lauritzen and me, and I told him some of the rumors—not all of them because I did not want to scare him. I said nothing about a guide because I did not want to raise his hopes either. He looked frail and was coughing horribly.

"If I could ask you to get me a blanket somewhere?" he looked at me hopefully. "If I had only listened to Mrs. Lauritzen. She wanted to pack some, but they seemed an unnecessary burden to me."

"I'll see what I can do," I promised. "Perhaps at the

First Aid station. They'll open later." First I was going to look around town.

I threaded my way through the corridors and inspected the classrooms. I was searching for sick people. The typhoid rumor worried me more than anything else. There had been an outbreak back home last winter. Many people died, and the hospital soon became overcrowded and refused to accept more of the sick. They stayed at home and people nailed signs against their doors: *Attention! Infectious disease. Attention!,* which scared off looting soldiers and the secret police and the inspectors from the housing authority, who otherwise would have jammed more refugees into your rooms. The sign was therefore quite valuable and people kept it up much longer than required. Father did not take ours down till Kruegers reported it to the police, who made him take it down. As punishment he lost his ration card for one month, which made life worse for all of us, because naturally he had to eat part of our rations. All the time mother went around in a white coat, nursing people, and five died in our house alone. It was dreadful.

But nobody seemed especially sick. People looked gray and dirty, but what could you expect after many nights on a transport, not much opportunity to wash or change, and not enough to eat for a long time?

I stumbled over rabbit coat dozing on the steps.

"Watch out," she cried. "Oh, I should have known it was you!"

The door to the yard was without guards. There was no quarantine yet, and we were free to come and go as we pleased.

13

rated the suburb from the town. I passed through a
stone gate and entered a fairytale street: half-timbered
houses, gabled roofs, cobblestones. The beams were
carved and painted, the windows brightly polished,
the streets swept clean. Comfortable curtains hid the
rooms. It looked so neat, so perfect, so undisturbed
and untroubled, as if there had never been a war. Not
a single bomb crater, and no blackened wood and
broken glass.

Another oversight. These houses would have burned
like fat in a frying pan. One incendiary bomb would
have been enough to make the whole town explode
and send it to hell in minutes. But it had been spared
and smugly disregarded the squalor before its gates.
The people on the streets were different: clean, well
dressed, rosy, their cheeks round, their hair combed,
their shoes buffed. Proper people for a proper place.
Maybe they would sell me a blanket—but the stores
were closed and shuttered.

"What is the matter? Why is everything closed?"
I had stopped the nearest people.

"It's Sunday," the woman replied and took note of
my smudged face, the sloppily braided hair—I had
smoothed the upper part with my fingers since the

comb had broken in the tangles—the spotted jacket, the crumpled skirt I had slept in for three nights, the rope that tied my boots. I bet she did not notice their good quality; she only saw the grime. The girl at her side wore white gloves.

White gloves and a snooty face. She took in my appearance just as her mother did, moving her eyes from my unkempt hair to the soiled boots, and just like her mother's, her expression told me clearly how disgusting she thought me.

I resented their staring. Yes, I had lost a button, I had not washed as often as I could. I had not combed my hair for some time and then it had been too late to comb through the snarls, but I was quite pleased. I had taken care of myself and the old people and I was trying hard to beat the odds against keeping our promise to Mrs. Lauritzen—I now thought of it as my promise too—and they, the townspeople, had not exactly prepared a warm bath for each of us at their school. Nor had they cleaned it up a bit and made it livable.

"Your parents should take better care of you, even if you apparently can't be bothered," said the woman. And the girl said, "It's Sunday and look how you are running around." The girl sneered more openly.

I kicked her against the shinbone and punched the woman's stomach with both fists. She staggered back and raised her pocketbook to whack it on my head. I grabbed her arm and tore the pocketbook away from her.

"Thief!" she shrieked and I slammed it into her middle.

"Clean up your filthy school first!" I screamed and ran.

"Stop the thief," she shrieked after me, and people turned and windows opened.

I ran through the crooked streets and slipped into the church by a side door. They would never find me here, if they had pursued me that far. The light filtered through stained-glass windows, creating islands of darkness. I could easily hide behind a bench, a pillar, or the altar. The one at home had been hollow and Wolfgang had spent one service there, or most of it. Till he sneezed.

He must have been allergic to incense. One of the altar boys had placed the censer right in front of him and Wolfgang had sneezed uncontrollably. He had sneezed and choked and sneezed, and the tears spurting out of his eyes blinded him. He had crawled out from under the altar, dragging the white starched sheets along and leaving Reverend Severin clutching the crucifix and the Bible and speechless for a long time. Then he had continued his service as if nothing had happened. Wolfgang had been wearing the brown uniform of the Hitler Youth, complete with armband and shoulder strap—father's present for his eighth birthday—and Reverend Severin had not dared to speak up against that uniform—or father. Next Sunday he preached about wolves in sheepskin, but perhaps he meant it the other way around, and Wolfgang went home all puffed up.

When I heard footsteps outside, I crept behind the altar and found a similar hole. There I crouched, sniffing the faint, familiar odor of incense and feeling quite safe, while someone walked around in the church.

I was not proud of my outburst. It was stupid to fly into a rage only because a total stranger says a few nasty words that remind you of your parents and how they had treated you. I must stop being that touchy. I was supposed to be in town to find a guide to help the Lauritzens and myself across the border and now all I did was take refuge in a church. I was wasting time.

The footsteps finally moved away; a door opened and shut. I slipped out of my hole and tiptoed to a door opposite and found myself in a serene and lovely cemetery. An empty cemetery with giant old trees and solid graves and ivy-covered walls and grounds. Moss padded the gravestones.

A lovely cemetery for Mrs. Lauritzen, if only she had not set her mind on the one in Cologne. It could not be prettier. But it was too late to persuade her now. Anyway, she wanted to be close to her daughter.

I wandered around deciphering the chiseled letters. Many people had died young—younger than I was— and I felt sorry about their short lives, just as I had felt sorry for Albert's brothers and sisters when his father shot them dead before the Russians came. It seemed such a waste because you aren't really able to do much before you are eight or ten years old.

Lots of men were killed in wars. *Died for the fatherland,* read the inscriptions.

"Hey you," a high voice piped and suddenly I was surrounded. "Looking for someone?"

"Yes," I mumbled, relieved they were not hunting for me. "My grandmother's grave."

Five pairs of eyes appraised me. "Must have died young. Last one buried here was in 1872. They've used the new cemetery ever since. When did she die?"

I calculated quickly. I could not let her die before mother had been born, so grandmother had to be alive way into this century. "Nineteen twenty-three, in the big flu epidemic after the First World War," I said. "So it must be the new cemetery." And I turned as if to leave.

"This is our meeting place. It's secret," piped the same high voice, and its owner, a small boy, was quickly jabbed in the ribs.

"Shut up," said the oldest of the group. "You talk too much. Paul always talks too much. But where are you from? You speak strangely."

"From the north," I said.

"What are you doing here? Besides looking at graves?"

"I came with a transport."

"Alone?"

"Alone!"

They moved closer and regarded me with sympathy and envy. "Alone! Are you an orphan?"

"Yes," I said simply. It had slipped out for the second time, but I felt the same as I imagined an orphan must feel: abandoned, resentful, angry, and sad and also pleased at being on my own—a queer mixture with one or the other feeling prevailing at different times. Right now I immensely liked being on my own and wouldn't have changed places with anyone, even for tea with crumpets and cake and sandwiches.

"Your family, are they all dead or have you lost

them?" The taller girl had put an arm around my shoulder.

With no pang of conscience I pronounced my father dead and my mother missing. I hesitated a bit over Wolfgang and then declared him lost with my mother; I did not have to lie about Jochen's fate. I told them about his last letter and that they had amputated his leg and that I was going to search for him.

They demanded the whole story. "Begin at the beginning," they said. "When did you leave your town? What happened first?"

These three boys and two girls looked more ragged than anybody I had seen in this town so far. They perched comfortably on the gravestones: Paul, the small boy, was snuggling against a statue of Death the Reaper with a rusty scythe. Their leader, a boy my age, spoke differently from the others, though they tried to imitate him. I thought I recognized his dialect: they were the local kids and he had been sent here away from the bombing of Berlin. Perhaps he knew about guides?

So I invented a big fat lie. As entertainment.

I told them I came from one of those big estates in the east, terribly rich with miles and miles of land stretching in all directions: forests and fields and villages and a beautiful mansion with lots of servants. Father served somewhere in the war and got killed in the winter of '43. When the Russians broke through the German lines a year later, mother had five horse-drawn wagons prepared, outfitted with stoves, covered with precious antique rugs, and filled with food and clothing, bedding, furs, our valuable paintings, and silver and jewels. The villagers prepared their wagons and together we trekked westward. The cattle were herded along. It was winter. I shuddered.

I did not have to fake the shudder. That winter had been extremely cold everywhere. I had blown holes in the ice that covered our windows and had watched more than one weary line of wagons trudge to the west. Few of them were as elegant as I have described ours, but many of the riders and drivers had been clad in furs.

I shuddered and the children shuddered along with me in the snowstorms, the icy, biting winds. We groaned about the miserable roads, the bomb craters, the abandoned vehicles, the dead animals, the unbelievable confusion and congestion, and the utter terror of the planes whipping down from the sky and emptying their machine guns into us.

People and horses and cows and dogs and chickens had been wounded and killed and left to be buried by the snow and ice. Wheels had broken and axles splintered. Sometimes the German soldiers fled along with us and sometimes they cleared us off the road and sped east for a new defense line. And there was the constant roar of the big guns. Today nearer, tomorrow farther away.

In a village I had strayed away from my family for a moment—why did I have to look in that window? —and saw them take one road, while an armored column pushed me into another. When I struggled back against the human current, they were gone. They could not stop for me nor turn around. The stream of refugees carried them westward. I never caught up.

"Then you don't know for sure that they are dead," they said, hoping for me.

"People from the village traced me and said they had been surprised by planes and machine gunned. They had seen what they thought were their bodies."

"Your father might come back. There were many false reports," said the smaller girl. "Mine did. We didn't expect him anymore."

"Mine didn't," said Paul.

"That was over a year ago," said the older boy. "Where have you been since?"

"An orphanage," I explained. "And it wasn't terrible. Till they discovered an aunt of mine in the British zone and now I am released into her custody. And she knows nothing about it!"

"So you are free to live on your own," stated the boy. "Nobody would miss you." He looked around at his companions and they smiled and nodded. "It's agreed," he said. "You can stay with us, if you want. We have quite a few secret places. And enough to eat!"

I was touched by their invitation and tempted to take them at their word. They had offered me a home without knowing anything about me but the tragic story I had invented and now was not particularly proud of. It would be fun to live with them.

Then I shook my head. "No. Thanks anyway," I said, "but I do have to go. How does one cross the border?"

14

"HE KNOWS IT BEST."
The other kids pointed to the older boy. "He crosses all the time. But why can't you stay?"

"I do go back and forth," admitted the boy and grinned. "I can understand that you don't want to stay here, but why don't you wait and cross through the checkpoint when it reopens? You do have papers, don't you? And they do give you something to eat at the school, don't they?"

"Not much," I answered, "but there is a problem." I paused and looked from one kid to the other and decided to tell them the truth. They would not think it was crazy to escort dead Mrs. Lauritzen across the border. They would not be scared of her or afraid that she might carry a disease or worried that her papers were invalid since they were made out to a live person. They sprawled on the graves as if they had been comfortable with death for a long time.

"I do need help," I began and immediately they moved closer and listened carefully. "It is not for me, but I promised . . ." and I told them the whole story from the beginning—the way they liked it. I covered the ugly incident at the platform at home, our end-less delay on the plain, her death during the second night, our further travels, and our arrival at their school. I portrayed the closet with the wheelchair sticking out into the corridor, where people pushed back and forth, and I repeated that Mr. Lauritzen was determined to keep his promise to bury her in Cologne, where she had wanted to rest near her daughter's grave. And I told them that he and I were willing to go to jail in the process and that he was old and rather shaky himself and coughed horribly. I left out the times that I had neglected him, but told them he would be lost without me and that I had made up my mind to see him through. And they accepted my story as quite ordinary.

"We see what you mean," they said. "It would make you feel like a pig to desert him."

"A crossing can be arranged." The older boy was thoughtful. "Tomorrow after school?"

"How about the wheelchair?"

"I never transported one before, but why not? The road is rough, but she won't feel the bumps, right?"

"And how much money?"

"Are *you* getting paid?" he asked icily.

I shook my head. I shouldn't have mentioned money. Now I had offended them. One does not pay for friendship.

"I am sorry," I stammered. "That man at the school, he wanted one hundred, so I thought . . ." and I didn't know how to go on.

"All right." He turned to his friends. "Tomorrow after school. Let's make it a picnic!"

"A picnic, a picnic," they cried. "Just as we did with the people from Leipzig!"

They decided to meet me and the Lauritzens not far from the Ernst Thälmann Elementary School at two o'clock with real food for a real picnic. I only hoped the school would not be placed under quarantine before then and inquired if it had happened earlier.

"Three times," they replied, which was not very reassuring.

The bells in the church tower rang.

"We have to break up," said the spokesman for the group. "Go with Louisa if you are hungry. They butchered a pig four days ago." Louisa nodded and smiled and took my arm.

"See you all tomorrow. And thanks again!"

We ran through narrow streets and stopped at a yellow house with broad green beams and green shutters. Louisa asked me to wait and disappeared into the doorway. A few minutes later she returned and pulled me inside, a finger on her lips. We tiptoed through the dark hall and into the kitchen, where the ceiling hung low and crooked. She listened and I listened too. I realized I was not exactly welcome by everybody. The whole house creaked and a wood fire in the kitchen stove flared. How could one hear anything? But Louisa seemed satisfied that there was no danger and closed the door.

She quickly inspected the cupboards and spread their riches on the table, things I hadn't seen for years: freshly baked bread with a shiny crust, real butter, sweet and yellow, sausages, cheese, a chocolate cake. My mouth watered while she sliced the bread, smeared it with butter, and heaped cheese and sausage on each side.

She poured milk in a pot and added chocolate powder and stirred it on the stove. I had not drunk hot chocolate for more than three years and the aroma made me swoon. While it heated up, she wrapped the sandwiches in a newspaper and handed me the package.

"I'll have more for the picnic," she said, and I felt as rich as the fat woman. "We always had enough to eat here, but people hate to share." I thought of the watery soup at the camp and the small piece of bread.

Now she filled a mug with hot chocolate. "Drink it!"

"Is that you, Louisa? Are you alone?" a woman asked from somewhere upstairs.

We stood frozen—the cup inches away from my mouth—and listened to the slap of slippers above. Then the stairs creaked under her weight.

Louisa motioned me to the door. "Run," she whispered urgently and then continued in a normal cheerful tone, "Yes, it's me and I am making a cup of chocolate. You want some too?" She had snatched the mug away from me and pressed a piece of cake into my hand instead. Reluctantly I crossed the hall with as little noise as I could. I didn't want to get her into trouble, but I was sorry to leave the hot chocolate.

Now Louisa started to sing, apparently the first song that came into her mind—or did she count on its effect? She burst into the "Horst Wessel Lied," the most famous Nazi song we all knew from marching, assemblies, and radio broadcasts.

"Cut that out!" I heard the woman scream. "Cut it out!" Her loud, upset voice muffled Louisa's singing and any sounds I might have made opening and closing the back door. Now I ran. I could well imagine the scene that was being played out in the kitchen.

"Cut it out! You know that song is forbidden! You will get us all into jail! If we hear you sing it again, we'll have to beat some sense into you!"

And Louisa, pretending not to understand: "But you sang it yourself last year! Remember, you paid me ten pfennig because you heard my voice above the others and you felt so proud of me. That's what you said! You and father and the whole town! What's wrong with this song?"

That scene would cover any trace of my visit. Quivering, Louisa's mother would never give an honest reason; she would shout Louisa down instead of explaining that the winner can not let the loser keep on singing about how he was going to beat the winner. Now we were supposed to sing the winner's songs.

I was sure that with a little more practice we would burst into the "Internationale" just as automatically. What did the Americans sing? And the British? The French, I knew, sang a gory song about blood soaking the fields. I whistled it. The melody was difficult and I got stuck after a few bars.

I clutched my package and stuffed myself with cake and marched through the town, the gate, and the suburban streets and into the yard of the Ernst Thälmann Elementary School. The doors were open and unguarded and Mr. Lauritzen was happy to see me.

"I was a little worried about you," he said. "You were gone such a long time." It must have seemed a long time to someone who was sitting alone, not daring to leave his post, though the hours had passed quickly for me.

When I told him about the kids in the cemetery and my arrangements for the next day, he patted my shoulder and his eyes filled with tears. Two big drops rolled through the white stubble on his cheeks and it was terribly embarrassing. I could not show him the package with food for fear he would break down completely and turn all gushy.

"You better get a shave," I said briskly, "or we will be too suspicious-looking in town. They are all so proper. By the way, do you know it's Sunday?"

"Mrs. Lauritzen and I used to promenade along the river bank on Sundays after church. There were boats on the water and outdoor cafes where we stopped for a beer. But you are right, I have not shaved for three days. Mrs. Lauritzen would never let me get away with that!"

I borrowed his comb and worked on my pigtails, but I guess I should have borrowed scissors. It was absolutely hopeless, so I braided them with all their tangles. Mr. Lauritzen looked nice and smooth when he came back, but how sunken his cheeks were! How frail his whole body! He would never last through a long march without food to build up his strength—as much food as I could get together.

"It must be time for dinner," I said. "I'll check the Mess Hall."

"Mrs. Lauritzen was quite a cook." The old man licked his lips. "You should have tasted her stews. And the cakes and cookies!"

The corridor to the Mess Hall was filled with angry voices.

"What the hell is going on? Why don't they open up?"

"What are they waiting for? We're starving!"

"Haven't you heard? They're closed till tomorrow!"

"You must be kidding, though I've heard better jokes before."

"It's true, all right. They don't open before the morning!"

Rudi wiggled to my side. "Let's break the door down!" he cried. "Let's break the door down!"

"He's right!" Others picked up the cry, "Let's break it down! Come on, all together, let's break it down!"

Rudi let out a shrill jubilant battle cry and he and I threw ourselves into the mob and pushed and shoved as hard as we could, till Frau Hasselmann reached out from behind, grabbed Rudi's neck, pulled him out of the crowd, and would not release him. I did not watch her slap him, but fought on until at last the door creaked under our joint charge and we streamed into the vast kitchen.

It was empty, with not even a drop of the last lunch's soup left nor a crumb of bread. They must carry every single bit home to feed their pigs. Only salt and vinegar sat on one shelf and I was just going to pocket a box of matches when the captain blocked my way and pocketed them himself and the fat woman barred me from reaching a tiny piece of soap at the sink.

"You don't look as if you use soap!" she chuckled.

People took spoons and knives and forks, cutting boards, a funnel, potholders, scraps of turnip. They turned the trash cans over and examined their contents, pulled at the drawers, walked away with the cook's apron and someone's rubber boots, smashed an old pickle jar in the middle of the floor, and poured salt and vinegar all over the stoves. The captain broke two windows with his crutch and unscrewed all the bulbs. I came back empty-handed.

"Close your eyes till I tell you to look," I said and Mr. Lauritzen closed his eyes while I unpacked Louisa's gift and displayed it on Mrs. Lauritzen's lap.

"Now!" I commanded. He opened his eyes and marveled at the thick sandwiches, the butter, the sausages, the cheese; we would not miss dinner as much as the others.

"Where does this come from?" he wondered. "How can they distribute food like this at the Mess Hall? I haven't seen such bread since the beginning of the war. Smell it! Just smell it!"

"They don't!" I laughed. "It's from my friends in town."

"Thank God for your friends," he said and I divided our treasure into four parts: the smallest for me because I had already had my share in cake, one for the old man, and one each for Frau Hasselmann and Frau Warnke.

"God bless you," said Frau Warnke and pressed my hand. She divided her share into three parts and passed them out to her three kids.

"She stole it in town," explained Rudi to his mother. "You should have let me go too."

"Never mind where she got it," said Frau Hasselmann. "Sometimes one can't afford to ask too many questions." She held the bread to her nose, breathed deeply, broke a small part off for Rudi, and devoured the rest.

I ate my part and thought of the mug of hot chocolate that had come so close to my mouth. Its aroma again filled my nose and it made me angry that the woman had to choose the worst possible moment. Couldn't she have waited till I had gulped it down? Would I ever get something as good again? Later I stretched out on the floor. Without blankets —not even for Mr. Lauritzen. Short of stealing, I had not been able to turn up a single one in the buildings, nor at the First Aid station. Still it was going to be a comfortable night with plenty of room for our legs. Using my bag as a pillow, I felt happy in anticipation of tomorrow's picnic. I hoped they meant a regular picnic with a tablecloth spread over pine needles and food and drink for all. I kept thinking of a red-check-ered tablecloth like mother's. Sometimes during the summer she would serve juice and cookies in the garden.

"Did you ever go on picnics, before the war, in Cologne?" I asked sleepily.

"Many, many times," said Mr. Lauritzen. "With a wicker basket and a bottle of wine, meat, bread, a cake, and a thermos of coffee. I always fell asleep in the grass—Saturday was a busy day at the store—and Mrs. Lauritzen tickled my ear with a blade of grass to wake me up."

15

"ALL EVACUEES WILL walk to the border checkpoint immediately. These buildings will be cleared by seven o'clock. There will be transportation only for the sick. Everyone else has to walk!"

I thought I was dreaming, repeating in my dreams the orders of the days before, but it was real enough when the first official we had seen so far stepped over our legs and barked his message into each classroom. "These buildings have to be vacated by seven o'clock. That is an order! All evacuees are directed to walk to the border checkpoint. No one but the officially sick and crippled and their immediate families will be transported."

What a crazy idea! How could they make everybody walk to the border? Who would carry the luggage? I thought of Frau Hasselmann and Frau Warnke and the fat woman and their boxes and bedrolls and suitcases. It was different to drag them a short distance the way we had yesterday, but the border was how many miles away? Did they expect us to leave our only belongings behind? Had they planned this forced march on purpose to get rich on our stuff? And how about the captain with his one leg? Was he supposed to walk?

"What shall we do?" asked Mr. Lauritzen. "What do you think? Shall we walk to the border or wait for your friends? I am all confused." He smoothed Mrs. Lauritzen's blanket.

I was not going to confess that I was confused too. Someone had to make decisions. "We will wait in the yard," I said. "If we catch the transport for the sick before noon, we'll take it. If not, we'll cross the border with my friends."

Though I would hate to miss the picnic.

The buildings buzzed with sounds of anger and frustration, and people seemed determined to hang on to their places. So after repeating the announcement several times, the camp official took other steps.

Suddenly local men and women with armbands swarmed in great numbers through the hallways and bellowed their orders. They closed in on one classroom after the other and in spite of the abuses they were bombarded with, they tossed the luggage in the hall and prodded and shoved and pushed the people outside, dragging the resisters along the floor. Not very gently. A man fought back and five officials overpowered him and hauled him away.

"We'd better get out on our own," I said and Mr. Lauritzen agreed. Then I piloted the old man and the chair out into the yard.

The whole camp population had assembled there in helpless rage and watched the stragglers, who received even rougher treatment: their baggage was thrown out through the windows and they themselves were kicked and knocked about. Then the doors and windows were locked.

It was cold and barely light. People waited for something to happen. They could not yet accept that there was no way out but to take the road to the checkpoint. On foot. With all their belongings.

After an hour or so a loudspeaker clattered alive: Under no circumstances would people be readmitted into the buildings. Rain was forecast for later in the day. There would be no further food distribution. Transportation was going to be provided only for the sick and their families. Who had vandalized the kitchen?

I made Mr. Lauritzen rest on our bags, propped against the fence. I wished I could wrap him in Mrs. Lauritzen's blanket—he needed it more than she. Coughing shook his body and he seemed to have lost some of his sureness. Again and again he asked me what we should do and he fussed around with the wheelchair. So I stuck firmly to my earlier decision to let time settle the question of how to cross the border: before noon with the sick the legal way, after noon with my friends the illegal way. Though I was torn. It was certainly better for the old man to take the fastest, easiest way across—which meant official transportation—and it was certainly safer for Mrs. Lauritzen to travel the illegal road. And personally I much preferred crossing with the kids.

Everyone cursed the local people who had kicked us out without dinner and breakfast. No wonder their town looked so prosperous and they so well fed. They must get rich on our rations as well as on our abandoned belongings if they made a habit of chasing hungry refugees on foot to the checkpoint. A cup of tea would have given Mr. Lauritzen some strength back.

The loudspeaker did not change its tune and slowly people became convinced that it made no sense to wait any longer. First only those with light loads marched off. By midmorning most were gone. Only the sick and the invalids remained, along with their families and some who hoped to pass as sick. Rabbit coat trekked out of the yard with the mousy man and his family and I never saw them again. But the fat woman squatted nearby on her many cases with the captain and we both watched her dig around in her bag. Would she come up with another hard-boiled egg?

Just then Frau Hasselmann changed her place and moved close to me and blocked my view. She had bundled up a perfectly healthy Rudi, his face now flushed with fever.

He looked through me with clouded eyes and mumbled: "Candy! Candy! Where is my box? I can't find it! I can't find it!" and choked and twisted while his mother slapped him to keep him quieter. I bet he was telling the truth. He had snatched my candy days ago, before we knew each other better. But what could I do now? Scream the way I had heard the fat woman scream? Would it help? I bent forward and saw the captain, smirking, peel himself an egg.

Frau Hasselmann offered to disguise me in the same manner. Two sick children would guarantee her transportation.

"I am with my grandparents. They are sick," I said and Frau Hasselmann seemed for a moment astonished but did not contradict me. "Why don't you borrow one of the Warnke kids?" She did.

Mr. Lauritzen looked suitably white and exhausted,

and the inert form of Mrs. Lauritzen, securely shrouded in her blanket with only an inch of white forehead exposed, presented a picture of total helplessness, as long as nobody discovered that all help was going to be too late.

Around eleven o'clock the locals descended on us after a final warning. Working in groups they started to sift through the remaining people. All wore armbands and all wore official faces. That's a face that shows no interest or feeling and you know its owner can't be persuaded to act like a fellow human being. He always is more important than you and always follows unbendable rules and regulations.

They sorted the people and forced many out of the yard. Apparently they were under orders to reduce our numbers considerably. No amount of crying or begging and pleading made them change their minds once they declared a person fit to walk. They were very thorough, inspecting bandages and feeling foreheads for fever. I worried about Mrs. Lauritzen. I worried so much that I was sweating all over. If they pulled the blanket away from her face, everything would be lost and she would never be buried in Cologne. It would break the old man's heart. Just when I had decided to play it safe and leave the schoolyard with the Lauritzens before the officials had a chance to question us closely, three trucks arrived.

The officials immediately gave up further questioning and ordered us—checked and approved or unchecked and perhaps totally disqualified—to board the vehicles. The open-back trucks were loaded deftly and they squeezed us all in: Frau Hasselmann and Rudi in his wrappings, the fat woman and her boxes, the captain, Frau Warnke and the kids, the wheelchair and Mr. Lauritzen and me, and many others. This time no one dared to complain about the chair. Minutes later we drove out of the yard.

I looked around for my young friends. I would have liked to have told them why I had left—only to spare Mr. Lauritzen the ordeal of hiking for miles—he was so weak—and to thank them for their willingness to help. I would have liked them to know how much I would miss their picnic. But school had not yet let out.

The trucks shook us mercilessly; the springs had been long gone. The road was no help either. Years of neglect in all kinds of weather had destroyed it, and the tanks and heavy military vehicles had churned the rest of the asphalt to pieces and dug deep holes. We bumped and skidded along and slammed into one another and against the rail. Yet people were silent. At least we were bumping and skidding on wheels while at the side of the same road our companions trekked from the school. They trudged along with their burdens and I cringed when our trucks hit an especially big pothole and splattered them with mud. But they were too tired to curse us aloud.

It did start to rain as they had forecast in the morning. A fine mist changed from tiny droplets into a steady thread of water and the open trucks gave no protection. At my side Mr. Lauritzen was constantly busy rearranging Mrs. Lauritzen. The shaking of the truck loosened her shawl or blanket, and the extreme jolts pushed her poor body almost upright or made her slump over sideways. And the rain made matters

worse by drenching her and her covers and she became more unmanageable. From time to time he gave
me an almost despairing look and I tried to drag her
body back into the correct position and fake a reassuring smile. She was getting heavier with all the
water. Fortunately people around us were too miserable themselves to pay much attention and Rudi, who
liked to comment on things other people prefer not
to mention, rode in the truck ahead.

"We must be almost there," I said. "It can't be much
longer." I don't know if I felt sick to my stomach because of the bumpy ride on an empty stomach or
because I dreaded the checkpoint.

Then we reached the border and I started sweating
again.

16

THERE WAS A DOUBLE
barrier across the road that closed it off. Barbed wire
stretched into the distance. Barracks loomed on both
sides, and the whole area swarmed with people and
their luggage and Russian soldiers and more Russian
soldiers.

They waved us to a stop. One truck waited in front
of us, the other pulled up behind. The rain dripped.
It fell on the soldiers who guarded us, five soldiers for
each truck. It fell on the people, who walked timidly

up to the barrier and presented their papers, and it fell on the guards who studied them. It had soaked the Russian flags that decorated the checkpoint. It had filled the holes and glistened on the road between our barrier and another one three hundred yards away: the British zone with its checkpoint, flags, barracks, barbed wire, and soldiers behind the no-man's-land.

"Are we at the border?" asked Mr. Lauritzen and peered into the rain.

I nodded stiffly.

"And what will happen now?" he continued anxiously. "I don't have much experience with borders. Once Mrs. Lauritzen and I took the train to Brussels and twice we walked up to the border just behind Aachen. They were very nice and polite and did not carry guns. But it must have been almost twenty years ago."

"They'll open the barrier and let us across," I said as cheerfully as I could. "You'll see, it will be a cinch." I wasn't at all sure of that.

"Perhaps we should have waited for your friends," said Mr. Lauritzen. "Don't you think it might have been safer?"

There was no answer I could give him.

We watched some people who were allowed to cross into no-man's-land, while others were turned away and directed to one of the barracks, where long lines of people waited, their faces pinched with fear. Singly they were admitted into the building and singly they reappeared after a long time, either escorted by soldiers and led to another barrack or free to approach the barrier once more.

If we could only avoid the investigation in the barrack!

˙ They had to discover the corpse. There had to be some regulation that your papers were only valid as long as you were alive. Dead people needed a different set of papers. Although they *had* married Frieda Greese to Hans Christian Duchow after he had been killed in action in North Africa—did they only make exceptions for war heroes?

In any case, an investigation in the barracks was dangerous. I could well imagine upturned suitcases and unrolled bedding and mattresses slashed for hidden jewels and seams of coats fingered carefully. The trouble was nobody knew what was allowed to be taken along and what was forbidden. There were no lists of rules, and if they existed, they probably changed from checkpoint to checkpoint and from day to day.

People had devised their own rules—sort of common sense rules—that not only applied to such special occasions as crossing a border, but to everyday life, where you had to be prepared to be questioned and searched at the railroad gates, in the streets, at work, positively after curfew, often while waiting for ration cards, sometimes at home. But people too had to break their own rules because it might be important *not* to leave a letter or a book or a photo behind. Or your only diamond.

One should not keep or carry guns, pistols, rifles, knives, swords, hand grenades, shells, bazookas, or parts of weapons. Mother made Wolfgang and me bury a fragment of the bomb that had almost killed us.

Or any medals earned in any of the wars, no matter how long ago, or bought at a dealer or clearly home-made.

Or any certificate, passport, identification paper, photo, letter, or news clipping that would fix you in a place and time which you would rather not be associated with. Father had burned every single photo that showed him in his uniform, his old passport, his letters from the front line, my honorable mention at the last Hitler Youth Sports Festival, Wolfgang's birth certificate, because the clerk who signed it was named Anton Hitler.

Or oil paintings from the Hermitage in Leningrad or the Louvre in Paris no matter how long their sale would support your life. Or anybody's crown jewels. Or mercury, and I had not the slightest idea why mercury. Or watches and radios because the soldiers were crazy for them.

One should not keep or carry lots of the same thing, like mountains of butter, piles of nylon stockings, cartons of cigarettes.

Or books. They might be the wrong kind, like Adolf Hitler's *Mein Kampf*. Or diamonds. Or money, large amounts of money. Or any foreign currency. Or . . . the list was endless, and it was easy to make mistakes.

Yet how could you trade on the black market, for example, without sufficient supplies? Or burn a document you might need later? What would I do in a new school without my old certificates? They would place me a grade or two back because of my size and would not believe me if I protested. Even though the real papers proved I had not lived in Cologne during that time, I had to take them along.

"Are your papers all right?" I asked Mr. Lauritzen.

"Naturally," he said, as if it had never occurred to him that at least half of us traveled under some false pretenses. "You know what I am worried about!"

We waited and watched. Mr. Lauritzen held onto my shoulder and pressed it painfully each time one of the soldiers shifted or talked. I thought of possible answers to possible questions and almost despaired. There was no explanation for Mrs. Lauritzen.

Suddenly I was slammed back and the same force thrust Mr. Lauritzen into Mrs. Lauritzen's lap. Our truck roared forward. A stop at the barrier—just long enough for us to scramble upright—then the barrier was lifted and we rolled underneath its red beam, past the red flags and the disinterested soldiers. Not one of them wanted to see our papers. They hardly glanced up at us.

"We made it," I shouted. "We made it!"

"But isn't there another checkpoint?" asked Mr. Lauritzen and tidied the blanket on the wheelchair. "If each side guards its border, it follows there must be two checkpoints. So we have not made it yet." He peered ahead.

He was right. There had to be another checkpoint. In fact we could see it. But now we rode through no-man's-land and I wished I could claim it: my own territory, my own country, between barriers, fences, and barbed wire. A funny-shaped country, three hundred yards wide and four hundred miles or more long. Ideal for cross-country running, bike racing, or motorcycle competitions. I would invent my own flag, write my own songs, and make my own laws.

We reached the end of my free country.

Soldiers in a different uniform—another shade of brown, another cut—lifted their barrier, and when it scraped the cab of the truck and we ducked our heads to avoid being hit, they howled with laughter. Otherwise they were not interested in us either. They did not ask for our papers; they did not order us into their barracks. Instead they waved us along a muddy road filled with other vehicles and people on foot. I wondered if they goofed off like this every day. Why did they stand guard if they let everybody pass without checking? Why keep the barrier closed? Just to amuse themselves? Maybe a border is not a border unless it can be closed from time to time. Maybe they were not interested in our papers, because they thought the Russians had checked us. It did not matter.

Mr. Lauritzen and I shook hands ceremoniously and congratulated each other. I was sure we were on our way to the station. We would catch a train, arrive in Cologne this very evening, and bury Mrs. Lauritzen in her cemetery tomorrow.

"That was as easy as years ago in Aachen!" exclaimed Mr. Lauritzen and all the weariness was wiped off his face. "Only these soldiers were less polite."

"Aren't you forgetting it took us four days to come this far?" said the fat woman. "By the way, where are we?"

I had no idea where we were. My geography is somewhat spotty, consisting only of places of battles that the German side had won. But why worry? The British checkpoint had been a cinch—so I thought.

17

BUT IT WAS ONLY THE
beginning.

We did not arrive at a station, but at another high wire fence with endless rows of bleak barracks behind it. The truck pulled through a gate and stopped abruptly, pitching us forward a last time.

"Get off! Quick! Quick!" shouted an official with a Red Cross armband. "There are more coming after you. We don't have all the time in the world. So hurry up! The sick line up at the first door, all others go over to the next barrack. So will you *hurry!*"

"Oh, no," groaned Mr. Lauritzen. "Not again."

"I told you so!" said the fat woman. "Isn't your wife lucky to sleep through all this!" She eyed the wheelchair enviously. "And to rest so comfortably all the time! Who would not like to change places with her!"

I steered Mr. Lauritzen and the wheelchair to the first door. It was impossible to tell if it was the right thing to do, but with such a chair and its occupant all but invisible I did not dare to queue up with the healthy people. Anyway, all of us stuck with the sick. So far it had served us well. It rained and the line moved slowly.

I don't know what I expected when the door finally

134

opened for us. Some sort of welcome perhaps, a cheer for making the long journey successfully, for coming home after a long evacuation. Instead someone gripped my neck and pushed the nozzle of a spray gun down between my shoulder blades and the sickening, sweetish foul clouds of delousing powder bellowed out from under my skirt. I fought vainly and another shot was aimed into my hair and filled my mouth, and a third was leveled down my front. It all happened so quickly I could hardly scream.

When I blinked through furious tears and the billowing clouds, I saw them pick up Mrs. Lauritzen's blanket and envelop her body in the foul powder. They worked in gas masks, ghostly efficient and without words. They sprayed the old man liberally and yanked us forward into a curtained hall, where we stood retching. But with nothing in your stomach, you can't get anything out.

Alone, I was pushed into a cubicle and blinded by its lamp. Someone told me to lift my jacket, blouse, and undershirt, and when I hesitated because he gave no reason and why should I undress for nothing, he barked:

"Go ahead! I am the doctor!"

How could I see his white coat and the stethoscope around his neck with my eyes still brimming with tears and his lamp in my face?

Now he came closer, stared at me and said with distaste: "Why do they all have lice!" With my watery eyes, I looked down my chest and saw nothing but traces of flea bites. Pretty old flea bites too. I was insulted because mother had searched my hair daily and had never found more than a couple of lice and my scalp did not itch, so I knew I did not have any—at least not a great number. But he acted as if they were crawling all over me.

I was going to protest when he went on sniffing. "Don't you ever wash?"

"Where?" I asked, and I was so mad I could have kicked him (but how would it help Mrs. Lauritzen if I lost my temper?). "The transport has not been exactly first class."

He should know the packed freight trains, the filthy camps, and muddy roads. If he worked here they should make him ride a transport just for a few days to teach him what it was like. Let's see how white his coat would stay. And he would learn the difference between lice and flea bites.

Catching a flea is not a matter of cleanliness or uncleanliness—it's more a matter of luck. They leap at you from the floors of schools, stores, churches, homes, movie houses, railroad cars, where they live in huge numbers in the cracks of the wood. The smell of soap—if you happen to have any—does not deter them. They want your blood. The skin swells up where they bite and suck, and it itches. Lice make you itch wherever they are and their bites don't show—maybe under a magnifying glass. Usually I could feel a flea wandering over my body between underwear and skin and capture it without stripping—few could do it—before it bit me once, but this one must have attacked me during the night.

Now the doctor asked a lot of questions and I shook my head without paying much attention. Yet apparently it was the right thing to do because shortly after, I was told to cover up again and was ordered into the next compartment, where they demanded my papers.

I had been thinking about the Lauritzens. If they confronted the doctor and his questions, they would be lost. What would happen if he wanted to see her chest? He would never understand that we had to bury her in Cologne because it had been her last wish, even though it ran counter to all the health regulations. Perhaps I could divert his interest by talking about possible typhoid at the Ernst Thälmann Elementary School; he seemed fascinated by dirt, odor, and disease.

"Grandfather has my papers," I said and slipped back into the hall just in time to grab onto the wheelchair before it was ordered into one of the doctors' cubicles. The same lice detector.

"Don't worry," I whispered to the old man. "Just follow my lead." And I wished with all my heart the doctor could be fooled.

He told me to lift my jacket, blouse, and undershirt and I obeyed a second time. He stared at me and he exclaimed again with a voice full of distaste, "Why do they all have lice!" and I tried to look crestfallen and thought if he can't remember that he saw me a moment ago and if he can't distinguish between fleas and lice, perhaps he won't notice the difference between alive and dead. It was worth a try. And we could always fake surprise that she was dead. So they never would be able to prove that we had taken her dead body along intentionally. We had crossed the border into the British zone without stopping and that had lulled me into believing the British did not check, examine, and question, but it seemed they were much better organized and more thorough than the Russians. They checked everybody, though I didn't know why. The medical examination was going to be Mrs. Lauritzen's toughest hurdle.

"Don't you ever wash?" He sniffed and instead of punching him in his smug face, I agreed pleasantly that I should wash more often and answered all his questions with a No. He was finished with me and stepped up to the wheelchair.

"Well, what do we have here?" he said.

"Grandmother here is a little"—I tapped on my forehead—"you know, crazy. If you examine her, she might get violent. It happens if one wakes her up. Not always, but most of the time."

"Doctors upset her," added Mr. Lauritzen severely. "You won't have to rouse her? There is nothing that she can tell you. She is not quite . . . you understand what I mean? Senile, you know. Senile. And she can be violent." He looked sad and concerned—for the doctor as much as for Mrs. Lauritzen.

"Is that so?" murmured the doctor and walked past the wheelchair to the sink in the corner and began to wash his hands.

"She fights, scratches, spits, and bites," I boasted.

"Sometimes, only sometimes," muttered the old man. "It's not as bad as she says."

The doctor was still washing his hands.

"She bit off Dr. Vogelsang's finger," I said triumphantly, "clear through. It dangled on a piece of skin. You wouldn't think she was that strong. But she is! And was he mad!"

"It *was* unfortunate," said Mr. Lauritzen. "But we warned him! We warned him."

The doctor dried his hands very slowly. Slowly he walked back to the wheelchair, his hands hovered a moment over the blanket—then he gave Mrs. Lauritzen's body a perfunctory pat and turned his full attention on the old man. He made him bare his chest—his skin fell in thin folds over each rib—and examined it closely. He knocked against the ribs with his fingers, squeezed them together, and released them and then made him breathe rapidly and slow down again. He ordered him to cough and, in obliging, Mr. Lauritzen coughed himself into a fit. The doctor slapped his back to halt the attack and only made it worse, so he pushed us into the next compartment to get rid of us.

"Papers!" they yelled.

I presented mine and, still coughing, the old man presented his. There was not even time to get worried that they might discover that some of my papers were forged. They were interested in nothing but our destination. They flipped through the rest of the documents and handed them back carelessly. And I was almost insulted: there we had gone through all the trouble and expense of bribing and forging and not once during the whole journey had anybody bothered to actually look at the papers. We should have eaten the butter and eggs ourselves. And I could have saved myself some apprehension.

"Cologne," they grunted. "A transport leaves tomorrow at 10:30." Then they passed me a bundle of papers and tossed a similar bundle on Mrs. Lauritzen's lap and yelled, "Next! Papers!" at the newcomers.

"But why can't we leave today?" I demanded. "We are already four days late!" "What difference will one more day make?" they replied. "The train leaves tomorrow!"

"But it's urgent," stammered Mr. Lauritzen between coughs. "It's urgent."

"That's what everybody tells us," they said. "What can we do? We have nothing to say about it! It's not our decision!"

"But where do we stay?" I continued. "And do we get food? We've had nothing to eat since yesterday noon!"

"It's all in the papers." They gestured at the bundle. "So they saved your rations back there? They must live well." They chuckled with appreciation.

We landed outside in the mud. The rain had changed back into a drizzle. Barracks lined the road as far as I could see. The camp must be huge so they liked to keep it filled. At least it was big enough to give us room to hide Mrs. Lauritzen.

Again Mr. Lauritzen and I shook hands ceremoniously and congratulated each other. We had cleared one more hurdle.

"Mrs. Lauritzen used to say that I was a bad liar," the old man said, smiling. "She never trusted me with officials. It was always she who claimed there were bugs in the flour or the weight was short on the butter shipment to get a little more for the people in our neighborhood. She would have been proud of me today."

140

So far life in the British zone of occupation did not seem different from what we were used to. They pushed you around in both places. Why hadn't they greeted us with a slice of bread and a bowl of soup instead of hitting us on the head with a beam, spraying us with the hideous delousing powder, and subjecting us to a stupid doctor? I might have been much more willing to learn their songs. I grabbed the papers before they slipped into the mud and studied them.

18

THREE TRAIN TICKETS, three meal tickets, three pieces of paper with numbers.

The train tickets said Cologne. They were regular ordinary brown train tickets and made me feel we had arrived.

Six meal tickets: dinner and breakfast for the three of us. Two people with three rations. We were rich!

The numbers read: barrack 143, bed 17, bed 18, bed 19.

Bed! How marvelous, how simply marvelous to put my head on a pillow, pull up the cover, and sleep on a mattress without fear that someone would step on my feet, hands, arms, legs. Mentally, I apologized to the British for not thinking much of them a second ago.

"They thought of everything: train tickets, food, beds," I said happily. "Let's find our barrack first," and I loaded the bags on Mrs. Lauritzen's patient lap and pushed the wheelchair through the slosh.

"Are you sure this is the right direction?" Mr. Lauritzen followed and his steps were slow and faltering. "The numbers seem to be getting lower."

So we turned around and I wished there were someone to help me with the chair. At the third intersection I spotted Rudi or he me. He started bragging immediately how everybody but him had been scared stiff at the border, that the barracks were comfortable, and why was I still dragging along with the old guy who made me do all the work?

"Can't he push his own wheelchair? What are you getting out of it?" he asked scornfully.

"I am going to get his family diamonds," I said. "They are hidden in his garden in Cologne. Hofweg 19. He told me the exact spot where they are buried."

I kept my voice very low and Rudi did not know what to think. Too many people had buried their family treasures. Suddenly he showed a concern he had never shown before.

"How can the old woman breathe under your bags?" he cried. "You are smothering her. Wait, I'll help you!"

I asked him for barrack 143.

"At the other end," he replied. "Too bad you are not with us. But did you tell the truth? About the diamonds?"

"Did you steal my candy?" His face went blank.

But he helped me push the chair till his mother's shrill voice called him back. It was heavy work. And all the way Mr. Lauritzen trailed behind.

Then I opened the door to barrack 143. In the gray light the room was bare, totally bare. There was nothing in it: no people, no beds, no chairs, no tables. Nothing but two rows of duck boards on the ground. Wooden grates five-inches high and as wide and long as coffins. Two neat rows the length of the building. They were set on the earth floor and where the earth had turned muddy from the water that seeped through walls and ceiling, they were covered with mud. One stove stood cold and lonely in the middle of the room. I checked the number and compared it again with the one on my papers. I had not been mistaken: it was number 143.

I took back my apology to the British.

Nobody could possibly confuse the boards on the ground with beds, yet they were meant to be beds; they were people's size and numbered. Near the far corner of the barrack I located "bed" 17, "bed" 18, "bed" 19. It was a joke.

The worst spot in a bad place. Our beds were positively floating. Rivers of water had softened the ground in a wide area, and the moment I stepped on number 17, the grate submerged partially and the brown slush bubbled between gaps and slopped over my boots. As if they needed another soaking.

"It's only for tonight," said Mr. Lauritzen bravely. He shivered and petted Mrs. Lauritzen. "One more night and we will be home. Perhaps . . ."

But I was already busy piling grates from the driest area I could find—one on top of another to create platforms for Mr. Lauritzen and me with a space in between for the wheelchair. Then I set to work rearranging the numbers, and Mr. Lauritzen and I dug the pins, removed the cardboard squares, and replaced them in a different order. The spare ones I stuffed into my pockets.

"Now we have to get something to eat." I surveyed our work and parked the wheelchair, feeling hollow and weak inside as if I had been pumped empty.

"Do you think it's safe to leave her?" Mr. Lauritzen secured the blanket.

I nodded. "Anybody will think she's asleep," I said. "If you don't come, they might not give me your portion."

Kids up the road directed us to the central square. "But you won't get anything before six o'clock," they assured us.

The drizzle had stopped. People congregated on the roads and filled the square. They crowded around two large bulletin boards. Kids ran around and between them and jumped over puddles and raced paper boats and dug canals and harbors with their mess tins. My goal was the barrack with the large Mess Hall sign and my only thought was to persuade somebody to redeem our tickets before I fainted from hunger. Later I would study the bulletin boards. Now I steered Mr. Lauritzen across the square.

"I can't," he sighed suddenly, almost falling over me and hanging over my shoulders with all his weight. Then his body jerked in spasms of coughing. I pulled all my strength together to hold him, scared that he would glide away from me into the mud and more scared that he was going to die. He could not leave me alone! I did not stand a chance of burying them *both* in Cologne!

"You have to go on," I hissed fiercely. "You have to

keep your promise! You can't let go now! A few more steps and there will be help."

He straightened a little and shuffled along with me. I held my arm around his waist to support him and his weight pressed down on me, but we did not stumble and fall. We gained the stairs to the Mess Hall and there he sagged down. I flew inside, ran along the closed shutters, knocked with my fists against them as hard as I could, and shouted at the top of my voice: "Grandfather is dying on the steps! Help! Help! He needs food! Won't somebody help?"

And again I raced along the line of the shutters, knocking and shouting: "Help! Isn't anybody going to help?"

My voice must have been convincing. One shutter opened a few inches. "Go away!" it said. "Soup at six o'clock. No exceptions!"

"It will be your fault if he dies," I cried. "It will be on your conscience for ever and ever."

The shutter opened wider and a round face appeared. "My fault? I only follow orders," it said. "Anyway, dying of starvation takes a while. But let me see!"

With a bang the shutter closed and a round little woman stepped through the door. I wanted her to hurry. What did she know about starvation? With her it would take months and months of fasting. No wonder she thought it a slow form of death. She wouldn't even know ordinary hunger.

She waddled outside, where a few curious people stared down on Mr. Lauritzen, bent over him, felt his pulse, and pronounced him alive.

"It's the delousing powder," she explained. "It does make people sick. I wish they would change brands again. But the old kind made people vomit right in their station and you bet they didn't like that a bit. Now they faint somewhere in camp. He'll come to in a couple of minutes."

She started to turn and I blocked her way.

"How can you be sure?" I insisted. "Maybe it's the delousing powder *and* hunger! We've had nothing to eat for twenty-four hours! How can you say he is all right!"

Mr. Lauritzen stirred and tried to sit up. His face was ashen and his eyes empty. The people dispersed. Stories like mine were boringly common.

"Twenty-four hours? Really?" The round little woman regarded me with new interest. "Twenty-four hours? Come along then."

I did not leave her side and walked right with her into the kitchen. While she heated water on the stove, I stuffed a hunk of bread, two onions, a handful of sugar cubes, and three cooked potatoes between undershirt and skin. The potatoes were boiling hot and I danced up and down, doing fancy footwork like a boxer to shift them around. Not with complete success.

Then I joined her at the stove and while she fetched a mug, I grabbed a breaded piece of meat—a porkchop perhaps—out of the pan and crammed it down the front of my blouse. The grease dripped along the skin of my chest and the meat settled on my stomach— but not for long. Because all the time I bobbed up and down to keep the potatoes from scalding me too badly and with me bobbed the onions, the sugar cubes, the bread, and the meat.

The little round woman, watching me with open curiosity, offered the mug with tea. "Is anything wrong?" she asked and I shook my head and bounced. "Keep quiet or you will spill the tea," she admonished. "I put real sugar in it." I could not stop bouncing and spilled a little of the tea. I thanked her and bounced out of the kitchen.

While Mr. Lauritzen sipped it, I clawed the potatoes out and transferred them into the pockets of my jacket and hoped she would not discover right away that she had been robbed. Not before we had time to vanish around a corner. Right now I had no chance to deny the theft: a large blot of grease spread over the bulge in my jacket and I smelled heavenly. So strongly, in fact, I was afraid of attracting a hungry crowd.

Mr. Lauritzen drank and the sweet, hot liquid revived him and changed his color from ashen to plain white. He sat straighter.

"Please, we have to disappear quickly," I whispered, putting down his mug. "I stole half the kitchen." The potatoes literally burned in my pockets.

He understood at once. He sniffed, glanced at the dark blotch of grease, and reached for my free hand. Getting up laboriously and holding onto my shoulder, he staggered with me toward the nearest corner while I clutched my middle to prevent the food from slipping. It was none too soon.

We had just rounded the corner when we heard her high-pitched scream—"Thieves! Thieves! Where are the thieves?"—and a long, unpleasant description of us and how I had sneaked into the kitchen.

She would not find us now. The camp was huge and

alive with people, none of them too eager to take the sides of the officials and hunt for us. So we traced our way back to 143 without special worry and found it still unoccupied except by Mrs. Lauritzen.

Here I passed Mr. Lauritzen his part of the loot—having cut everything neatly in halves—and we both devoured it, including the raw onions, which forced tears into our eyes, and I licked the grease from my stomach. With the help of my fingers.

"You know, I am a thief," I said, astonished at myself. I had never before in my whole life stolen anything and yet in the kitchen I had acted with ease and assurance, as if I had done it many times. It had seemed the right thing to do. And now, when I should feel disturbed about it—because isn't it wrong to steal?—I was not at all upset. In fact, I felt rather pleased. And a lot less hungry.

"I think you probably did it for me," said Mr. Lauritzen gently and now his cheeks were faintly flushed. "I have been great trouble for you."

"If that were true, wouldn't I have given all the food to you?" I brushed him off. "But I ate my share and I don't regret it."

"For many years Mrs. Lauritzen sent two loaves and ten pounds of potatoes to the Bendlers and the Roslankys every week. They were poor and could use something extra. How angry we were when we thought that Walter, the Bendlers' boy, had stolen the chocolate hearts and how terribly ashamed when we fished them out of the barrel with herrings and realized that we had blamed an innocent boy. But we had never told him or his parents that we thought he was guilty. From then on, Mrs. Lauritzen always sent a bag of sweets along."

The old man, leaning against one bag, rested on his pile of grates and closed his eyes. He did look very tired and I was not going to bother him by asking him to explain what he had meant in telling me about the Bendlers' boy. What was his point? That I shouldn't have stolen from the one person who had been rather nice? Or that the round little woman in the kitchen should have shared more than her tea with us? That it was sometimes right and sometimes wrong to steal? I would ask him tomorrow if it seemed important then. Right now it really didn't. I was only wondering when I would do it again. And I did not have to wait long to find out.

19

FIRST I WENT QUITE openly to collect our soup and bread for the evening meal. It was a funny kind of bread that smelled and tasted sweetish and sort of rotten. It was made of very yellow flour and crumbled easily; they must have made it with sand, ground roots, bark, or something like that. Not like our bread in the Russian zone, where the flour was mixed with potatoes, wood shavings, sawdust, straw, and other unidentifiable matter that settled in distinct layers. Their bread had the same consistency through and through and was very different, though their soup could have come from across the border: water, a few cabbage leaves, potato cubes, bone splinters, more water. I had gone without qualm because I had figured on blending into the crowds.

Then I walked back and studied the bulletin boards. One listed tomorrow's transports, one to Cologne and one to Hamburg. Its other side was covered with camp rules, which I skipped. It was unnecessary to know them, since you were always told immediately if you came close to breaking one. Also, they changed too often and they might keep you from doing something sensible but forbidden.

The second board was filled with messages of people looking for other people and I read through them to perhaps find another soldier who had stayed at the same hospital as Jochen. No such luck.

"Are you looking for someone?" Rudi, sneaking up on me, asked. "I thought they were all dead!" He was tactful as always.

"My brother Jochen," I said curtly. "What's your barrack like? Ours stinks."

"Remember the fat woman?" he replied. "We were lined up behind her and when she passed a package over the desk, I made sure they knew I had seen them accept it. So we got the same slips for the same barracks. Bunks with mattresses, blankets, and pillows. Only she has two bunks for herself. It's number 37. Sort of special."

"Maybe I'll move in tonight," I said.

Wandering along the muddy roads, I peered into

windows. I saw rows of double bunks without blankets or pillows. I also saw a few barracks just like ours with wooden grates on the bare ground. If Rudi had spoken the truth, his place was really exceptional.

I wondered who had lived in the camp before us: political prisoners, communists, socialists, and others, jailed because their opinions about government were different from Hitler's. Or prisoners of war. Or people deported from Poland, Russia, Hungary, France, and other countries; millions had been forced to work in German factories for our war effort with our soldiers guarding them. The fence around the camp, topped off with barbed wire, looked grim.

When I returned to barrack 143, where we were still alone—and I couldn't decide if it was just an error or if they had assigned us to the worst place because the doctor wanted to pay us back for some of the discomfort we had caused him—we tried to sleep. But how can you sleep when your neighbor moves restlessly and coughs worse than ever and you know he is cold and weary and sick?

The sharp edges of my grate tortured my back and the cold was terrible. It attacked me through my damp jacket, froze my legs, and turned my feet numb inside the drenched boots. I envied Mrs. Lauritzen, who did not feel the cold and did not suffer, and I thought again of borrowing her blanket. But it was soaking wet from the rain and would not warm either of us.

I marched up and down the aisle and stamped my feet and slapped my arms around myself, feeling stupid. It did not do much good. Nevertheless I persuaded Mr. Lauritzen to march and stamp with me; father used to swear by it. But he soon tired.

"We should try to light a fire!" I said. "If only the captain hadn't kicked me away from the matches."

"There must be some in my coat pocket," said the old man. "Mrs. Lauritzen asked me to always carry them with me in case of blackouts."

He found them and some paper. So we tried to tear apart a wooden grate as fuel for our stove. The exertion made Mr. Lauritzen dizzy and brought on another horrible attack of coughing. I dragged him back to his grate, where he lay exhausted and trembling. If he lay here all night with nothing to protect and warm him but his rain-soaked clothes, he would be deadly sick by tomorrow. And we had come so far together. I could not let anything happen to him now.

"If I can't make it," he whispered and his teeth chattered, "I know you'll get Mrs. Lauritzen to Cologne. It's Central Cemetery."

"Don't talk that way," I said and swallowed hard, but the lump in my throat would not disappear. "You'll make it. I'll go fetch blankets for us."

The road was deserted. A row of street lamps gave a feeble light. It was probably one of their camp rules: curfew by nightfall. But I did not mind the risk. I kept thinking of the old man shivering on his grate above the mud and losing hope, while lots of other people were sleeping in soft, warm beds with full stomachs and dry clothes and I felt cold and angry and ruthless.

As I crept along the walls, I wondered if at this camp they started shooting without warning when they discovered you outside after curfew. During the war the Nazis shot without calling first, and later the Russians picked you up and threw you in jail for any length of time. Now I knew nothing about British customs. I wouldn't mind a night in jail; it could not be more uncomfortable than our present shelter, but I could not afford it on account of Mr. Lauritzen. On the other hand I did not want to die for a blanket, while he might die without one.

So I was careful and remained in the shadows of the buildings and leaped swiftly over crossings and pressed myself into the ground with every suspicious sound. I did not encounter a guard and after quite a few detours reached my goal: Barrack 37. The door opened without a squeak. I stood motionless and let my eyes adjust to the dim light. The air smelled of too many bodies—stale and thick, yet pleasantly warm. I tiptoed noiselessly along the aisle and glanced into strange faces. People snored and tossed, murmured or lay quietly hidden under piles of covers. I looked for an empty bunk, but when I found one, the additional blankets had already been removed.

Without hesitation I cast about for a likely candidate and stopped at a bunk whose occupant had lumped his blanket around his legs. Why should he keep it if he was warm enough without it? I worked stealthily, tugging gently at one corner and freeing it gradually till at last I held it all. He did not notice that it was gone; he muttered in his sleep and turned over.

I was so pleased with this maneuver that I looked right away for another victim. A woman nearby snored on her back, mouth opened slightly, two blankets draped over her body. Why should she have two, when others had none? What entitled her to a soft bed and a pillow while Mr. Lauritzen froze on his grate?

I got hold of a corner of her blanket and tugged it off her. I was forced to drop to the floor the very same moment, while the woman sat up in her bunk and groped blindly for her blanket. Her wandering hand touched my head twice, so I pushed the blanket into her hand, and with a sigh she fell back. That was close.

I crawled past the fat woman, enveloped in white blankets, and halted at another figure, partly uncovered in her bunk. Cautiously I peeled one of her three blankets off and she did not stir.

I did not attempt to steal Rudi's or Frau Hasselmann's, though they both had more than one; instead I picked a third blanket off their neighbor. I wanted four, two for Mr. Lauritzen and two for myself. While I was tugging at my last blanket, something cold touched my shoulder. I stiffened and waited for the clasp of a hand and an unfriendly voice demanding to know what the hell I thought I was doing. It came promptly.

"Hey you," it said and the hand kneaded my back painfully. "I guess you are trying to climb into the wrong bunk. That one is already occupied."

It was the captain's brash voice. So he too had bribed his way into the best-equipped barrack—bribed, or blackmailed like Rudi. I twisted out of his grip before he had time to turn me around and to realize who I was and that I had no business at all in this room.

"Excuse me." I sounded sleepy and kept my face averted, backing away from his bunk. "You're right, mother's is farther up," and hurried with my load along the aisle. I did not have the nerve to take the fourth blanket away with me, not when he started saying: "Wait, don't I know . . ."

Somehow I couldn't get past the fat woman: her pillow gleamed white and her blankets seemed softer than all the others. Her head nestled against the same cushion I had envied her every night on the transport, the mattress sagged under her weight, and the warm covers sheltered her big body. Here she lay so well cared for, while Mr. Lauritzen shivered without mattress, pillow, or blanket.

So I snatched the pillow from under her head, grabbed a blanket, and ran. And I had reached the door before there were any cries of protest. Nobody stopped me. Nobody stopped me on my way through the camp, although I could be neither fast nor careful with my load. Four blankets and a pillow are quite a lot to carry.

Mr. Lauritzen did not ask where they came from. He let himself be wrapped up like a baby, sighed with pleasure, snuggled into the fat woman's pillow, and fell asleep. I watched him for a moment, satisfied that the night would not harm him, then I rolled myself into my blankets and slept too.

20

in the morning. His cheeks were rosy and his eyes bright, yet he was content to let me fetch breakfast—he hardly touched his—pack our bags, and push the loaded wheelchair to the station. He followed slowly and paused often.

The station was nothing but a single track of rails bordering the camp. One train stood waiting, a real passenger train with normal coaches and an engine that blew steam. British soldiers with rifles paced up and down, and great numbers of German railroad personnel in their blue uniforms watched our arrival. As we filed through a hole in the fence, they checked our tickets and from time to time dispassionately pulled people out of the line and sent them over to the British, who escorted them back into one of the barracks. More questioning? More searching?

Again it was impossible to tell why they picked one person and not another. Perhaps Mrs. Lauritzen under her wet, heavy blanket would arouse their suspicion because her forehead was no longer white. There was no way to shield her, so I held my breath.

One official told Mr. Lauritzen and me to follow him, but instead of handing us over to the British, he showed us to a special compartment in the middle of the train marked "For Travelers With Unusual Luggage." Which made me laugh against my will.

He even helped us to lift the wheelchair inside and, bending over the quiet person in it, he asked politely if she liked to ride with the train or against it.

"She always prefers to ride with the train," replied Mr. Lauritzen with dignity, covering for my nervous laughter. "Don't you, dear? That way one knows where one is going. And we will see the spires of the cathedral of Cologne the moment they appear above the horizon. How we have longed for their sight! Isn't that right, dear?"

"They evacuated us three years ago." I had pulled myself together, but the official was no longer interested in us and walked back to his post.

The compartment was roomy, with ample space for the wheelchair, benches for the old man and me, and a rack for our bags. I had reluctantly left the blankets behind, though they were quite valuable, but the fat woman's pillow had been irresistible and now I begged Mr. Lauritzen to sit on top of it to conceal it. Obediently he sat down and closed his eyes.

Then I leaned out the window to watch the people and I grinned down on the ones I recognized from our transport. The captain hobbled past in a group of ragged former soldiers. The fat woman with all her boxes headed for my compartment—again she had found and probably paid somebody to help her carry them—and ordered: "Open the door!"

"It's for people with unusual luggage," I pointed out, "like harps, baby carriages, skis, coffins, fishing rods, and wheelchairs."

"What's that nonsense?" she cried. "Open up!"

Stubborn, I shook my head. I had no desire at all to travel with her. She signaled for an official and flushed with anger when he too directed her to another car. I could not help grinning more broadly.

"Watch out, brat," she hissed and waddled off.

Frau Warnke and her kids came along and they called, "How are you? How is Mrs. Lauritzen?"

I told them that she was as well as could be expected after such a long and wearing journey and that the old people were both looking forward to reaching home in a few hours.

"Finally home!" sighed Frau Warnke.

"Or what's left of it," shouted Rudi, who would have liked to climb in with me if he and his mother had not been ordered farther along. I was glad because with Mrs. Lauritzen and the state she was in this morning, it was much better to stay as far away as possible from people who had known us before. I wasn't sure but I thought I detected an awkward stench in the compartment.

Fortunately the only other person they allowed to join us carried two pails full of sauerkraut and an enormous trumpet—at least I assumed there was a trumpet in the black case till I thought of lots of other things that could be conveniently hidden in there— and he was profoundly apologetic about the odor of the sauerkraut. Which I didn't mind at all.

"Don't you worry," said Mr. Lauritzen and sniffed with appreciation. "We are used to sauerkraut, Mrs. Lauritzen and me. We carried it in our store. Excellent homemade sauerkraut just like yours. Tell me, did you use a little wine?"

The train left almost punctually.

"White wine," said the man with the trumpet, "and juniper berries, naturally."

"Naturally."

He offered us a handful and it tasted delicious. I don't mind sauerkraut right after breakfast—I don't mind anything to eat at any time. Mr. Lauritzen and our companion chatted for a while about the merits of different methods of sauerkraut production. Then they both lapsed into silence and the steady movement of the train rocked them into sleep. I had time to think.

Time to think about what I was going to do after we had buried Mrs. Lauritzen, which should be accomplished by evening. I pictured in my mind our arrival at the station in Cologne, a long march with the wheelchair to Central Cemetery, where we would persuade the attendants to help, her burial near her daughter's grave with me and the old man throwing earth on the coffin. I couldn't see further. I couldn't think of me shaking Mr. Lauritzen's hand and saying "good-by" and walking off back to the station, where I would find shelter for the night. Or me climbing a train south in search of Jochen. Or teaming up with a gang of kids. Or trading on the black market. Or taking a private look at the school where mother and father had enrolled me. And disliking it. My mind sort of stopped at the scene in the cemetery, and I just could not imagine myself leaving the old man alone next to the open grave and walking off. Walking off for good.

So I gave up thinking about it and cleaned my boots

with paper and a dry corner of Mrs. Lauritzen's blanket. Then I looked out the window into country I had never traveled in before.

The hills became less and less steep and finally spread into flat fields with well-kept farms and large barns. Every inch of the ground was weeded, ploughed, and fresh with winter wheat. So either people were less hungry and therefore better off in the British zone or else they had been forced to weed and plough and sow for the British. Perhaps mother was right and you did receive the full amount of food from your stamps.

Later we rolled through cities and towns and it was easy to understand why people had been evacuated and hard to understand why anybody wanted to return to places like these, where everything was destroyed. Except that it still was home.

For miles and miles and miles I could see nothing but bombed and burned houses, torn and twisted trees, craters, demolished bridges, wrecks of factories, rubble, and ruin. A wasteland. And people back home thought they had been badly hit!

The train traveled without halt and there was no end to the destruction outside. I wondered where Frau Hasselmann was going to live—and Rudi? And Frau Warnke and her kids? Wasn't it too cold to camp under the sky without a tent? And the fat woman? How could the contents of her boxes buy her shelter if there was no shelter? And the captain and rabbit coat and the mousy man and the thousands of other people? Would the old man find only blackened walls? How could mother and father have tried to make me believe in a school with white gloves and tea in the afternoon—tea and cake and crumpets? How could they have believed it themselves?

I was startled to hear Mr. Lauritzen's excited and happy voice: "Over there, look! St. Sebastian's mine!"

"And the smoke stacks of the Menzer factory," cried the man with the trumpet, and he nudged me in the ribs. "We are almost there."

How could they rediscover once familiar landmarks in the ruins? To me it seemed all the same, one big field of bricks and beams and holes and rusty iron. But they went on calling names as if the sights had barely changed.

"The station of Leverkusen."

"St. Georg's football field."

"Remember that line of poplars?"

"Droste Hagen's brewery!"

The old man noticed my silence. "Don't you recognize anything?" he asked. "Or are you so excited about seeing your family, your father, that you cannot talk any more?"

"There is no one waiting for me in Cologne." I blurted out the truth. "I have never been there in my whole life and I wouldn't be going there if mother and father had not sent me away. They no longer wanted me at home!"

"I do not wish to think badly of your parents," said Mr. Lauritzen, "but I find it hard to understand how one can send a child away."

"You mean you don't know each other?" the man with the trumpet pointed from me to Mr. Lauritzen to the wheelchair and back to me. "What the hell is she doing on this transport? I thought you belonged together!"

"We do belong together," said Mr. Lauritzen, and he put his arm around me. I did not shake it away.

We drove into a station, braked, and stopped. A battered sign read *Cologne*. I leaned far out of the window to catch a glimpse of the cathedral and couldn't see it.

"The bridge across the river Rhine is still under construction," barked the loudspeaker. "People on this transport will be ferried to the other side in good order. Please wait in your compartments till you are called." That explained the missing cathedral.

Railroad officials crowded the platform along with British soldiers and police and people with Red Cross armbands and others with yellow crosses. A regular reception.

"Welcome home," barked the loudspeaker in an afterthought. "Welcome home!"

"We are home," I cried. "We made it!" I hugged Mr. Lauritzen and hugged the wheelchair and could have danced around the compartment if there had been enough room. Mr. Lauritzen smiled and clutched my shoulders and I was afraid he was going to kiss me, but just as he bent down, the door opened and we were told it was our turn to unload.

"Can we help you with anything?" they asked and insisted on helping us—the railroad officials, the red and yellow crosses. Police and soldiers watched.

They lifted the sauerkraut, the trumpet case, and the wheelchair onto the platform. And me and Mr. Lauritzen. They loaded our bags on a buggy to cart them down two blocks to the ferry. They wrapped their arms around Mr. Lauritzen to support and guide him to the boat. They almost wrenched the wheelchair away from me and I could just prevent one Red Cross lady from stuffing the fat woman's pillow under Mrs. Lauritzen's head by screaming: "Leave my pillow alone, you old hag!"

She backed off, insulted, and I grabbed it out of her hands. So I steered the wheelchair down the street to the boat.

It was a small, open, flat barge. Behind it the river stretched wide and surged around the wreckage of the bridge. The city of Cologne rose on the other bank. Some people on the bank and in the boat were weeping as they stared at their city. I thought it would be easy now to sort people with forged papers from people who had come home.

Mr. Lauritzen wept and I did not weep.

Frau Hasselmann wept and Rudi sniffled.

The fat woman did not weep; she ate another sandwich.

Frau Warnke and her kids did not weep.

The captain wept. Not much, but he wept.

It seemed as if the cathedral was the only erect building.

"They smashed it up good," remarked Rudi. "I wonder how deep you have to dig for your family jewels?"

"Diamonds," I corrected him.

He stayed close to me as they herded us onto the barge and ferried us across. More people awaited us on the other bank—more soldiers and officials with all sorts of armbands and police. I was just a little wary about people from the school and, half hiding behind the wheelchair, scrutinized them carefully. If they should still be expecting me—though I doubted it very much after our five-day delay—they would not think of me in connection with an old couple or another kid. Too bad that some Red Cross busybody clung to Mr. Lauritzen at the other end of the boat, pretending to hold him up. As if he needed it now that we had arrived.

They told us to disembark; people first, luggage second. The Red Cross official was leading Mr. Lauritzen up the bank when I took my turn between people and luggage. The landing was high and many were willing to help hoist the wheelchair off the barge. Far too many.

It tilted to the right and Mrs. Lauritzen's body sagged with it to the right. The chair swayed to the left and with it the body. It was still stiff.

"Hold my hand," cried Frau Warnke up on the landing. "Don't be scared, we won't let you fall!" And with helpless horror I watched her reach for Mrs. Lauritzen's hand under the blanket. I was sure she would scream. And who could have blamed her for it?

But she did not. She froze, her face went completely blank, then her eyes widened and she looked down at the motionless form under the blanket with sudden understanding. She did not even withdraw her hand. "There you are," she said soothingly when the wheelchair was safe on the landing. "That wasn't so bad, was it?" Her voice trembled just a little. Her eyes searched for mine to let me know that it certainly was bad, but at least some of our troubles would be over now that we had reached Cologne.

I could have hugged her! Yet I never got the chance. When I scrambled on the landing, the fat woman discovered her missing pillow under my arm.

"Police!" she cried. "Get the police!"

And all the officials lifted their heads to find out what was the matter and two policemen stepped closer.

"Take her away! Hurry, hurry!" Frau Warnke said to me in a whisper. "I'll handle things here!"

There was no time to thank her. I took hold of the wheelchair and pushed it along, sideswiping the fat woman as she tried to block my way. The captain raised his crutch to stop me and I almost knocked him down. My only thought was to get up the bank and far away from the landing as fast as I could.

Behind me Frau Warnke's voice rose to a loud wail that muffled the fat woman's complaints. "My little girl! Where is my little girl? Who has seen my little girl? She's gone! She's gone!"

Other people joined in the chorus. "Who has seen a little girl?" Police and officials started looking immediately for the youngest Warnke kid, who had been clinging onto Frau Warnke's coat all the time. What a great trick to let me escape!

When I reached the top of the bank, I could not find Mr. Lauritzen. For one terrible moment I thought he had turned back to stand up for me against the fat woman and the officials. Then I saw him head with firm steps toward the cathedral. He did not even look around.

I tore off in the other direction, away from the cathedral. How he must trust me, leaving me like that! I hoped he knew about the hole behind the altar. I hoped he wasn't foolish enough to go back for our luggage. I still had my money and the clothes I wore, my boots and the fat woman's pillow, and he his pants, jacket, shirt, and coat. And we had Mrs. Lauritzen. She was safe! That was the important thing.

He was right to trust me, he was *right*. And I followed a trail through the ruins.

21

I FOLLOWED ONE TRAIL and then another and another and pushed the wheelchair along the broken ground till I was out of breath and so exhausted I had to sit and rest. But by that time there was quite a distance between me and the landing. Judging by the silhouette of the cathedral, I had worked my way around it in a wide half-circle and the danger of being caught had passed.

It had been close at the landing. Terribly close. I had been waiting for Frau Warnke to scream. Instead she had not only kept her composure but also had helped me escape from the fat woman and the officials. It had come as a complete surprise. But now I remembered that Frau Warnke had never spoken harshly, that she had asked after the old woman and offered her help many times. And I had thought of her as one of the others!

Though now they could not have avoided burying Mrs. Lauritzen in Cologne, there was no guarantee that they would have buried her where she wanted to be buried if we had been seized. And everything—our long struggle to keep the promise—would have been in vain. On top of it we would have lost our freedom: the old man would have been in jail and I at the boarding school. Somewhere in Cologne I would meet Frau Warnke again and thank her.

I sighed with relief and looked around. The rubble and ruin appeared not at all bleak but quite hospitable. And very much lived in. Just as in Magdeburg, people had built ingenious shelters in the wreckage; smoke curled from various unlikely holes and it smelled of soups and stews and reminded me of my empty stomach. It was time to get Mrs. Lauritzen settled and start making a living—by whatever means I could muster.

"Where is the cemetery?" I asked the first kid in the neighborhood. "Is it far?"

"That depends," was the answer. "If you want South Cemetery or Central Cemetery or . . ."

"Central will do," I cut the kid short. How many cemeteries did they have?

"That one is around here." And he told me how to get there.

I memorized his directions and pressed on. For someone as hungry and tired as I, it was far enough.

Mr. Lauritzen rose from the stone bench at the gate of Central Cemetery and his face glowed with pride and happiness. "I knew nobody would catch up with you," he said, "but what troubles for you, while I simply walked through the cathedral and out the other side and came right here! I kept thinking of what Mrs. Lauritzen would have done in my place and I was convinced she would have come here. Though I felt very bad letting you face the people alone. Tell me, would I have made matters worse?"

I nodded. He had worried, or he wouldn't talk so much now. "But I was not alone," I said. "Frau Warnke helped me."

"To think that someone from the transport would help us," mused the old man. "Yet she always inquired after Mrs. Lauritzen."

"We have to get on," I said and together we pushed the wheelchair through the gate. "Where is your grave?" I asked and was amazed how precisely the bombing had stopped at the walls of the cemetery, almost without disturbing the large old trees, the marble monuments, and clean rows of light gravel paths. Some broken limbs, the depressions of a couple of craters filled in, a few crosses and angels smashed —that was all.

"It's on our left," replied Mr. Lauritzen, "but you can't be thinking of digging it yourself? They won't let us, even if we had a shovel."

So we walked into the gate house for help.

"We've come to bury grandmother," I said. "Grandfather owns a plot here."

"CCP 368," said Mr. Lauritzen, "by the name of Lauritzen."

"Where are the papers?" demanded the attendant.

Mr. Lauritzen searched his pockets, found an envelope, handed it over, and the attendant studied its documents.

"It says nothing about a body," he complained. "Don't you know you need a death certificate? Signed and stamped?"

"You can see for yourself that she is dead!" I pulled the blanket from Mrs. Lauritzen's face and he hardly gave her a glance. It was nothing new to him.

"Makes no difference to me," he said. "I am just telling you the regulations. Rules are rules, you know that. Besides, only the certified dead are issued coffins. And you wouldn't like her to be put under like that?"

I looked at Mr. Lauritzen and Mr. Lauritzen looked at me and we both wanted a coffin.

"Couldn't we buy a coffin?" I played dumb. "I do have money."

"Money doesn't buy you anything these days," he said and gently stroked a black casket near him. "Money isn't worth much."

"My wedding ring?" Mr. Lauritzen pulled the narrow golden band off his finger and held it out. The attendant had his eyes glued on Mrs. Lauritzen till the old man took her ring off and passed them both over.

The attendant weighed them and inspected us from head to toe. "Is it warm?" He fingered Mr. Lauritzen's coat and I wanted to slap his hands away. "No, I guess not. You can keep it."

His hands touched the jacket, the pants, the shirt, traveled over my blouse and skirt, paused at my boots. I did not flinch.

"Haven't seen boots like these for years," he said.

"Real pretty, real, real pretty. Didn't know there was such quality around. Now, *they* might buy you a nice funeral."

I unlaced them and tossed them over to him. "Flowers?" I asked.

"Give me the pillow and I'll see."

I gave him the pillow. "Music?"

"I'll try for the wheelchair!" He picked up the body and deposited it casually into the black casket with the silver hinges and closed the lid. "The funeral will take place in an hour," he announced with sudden formality. "We will see you at the burial site." He walked off with my boots, the wheelchair, the fat woman's pillow, and the rings.

We went back to the bench to wait.

"I don't know how to thank you," said Mr. Lauritzen and his voice almost broke. "I wish Mrs. Lauritzen were here. She was always so much better than I in saying the right words. So you must excuse me." He coughed.

"It was just a game to see if I could beat the odds." I brushed him off and could feel the blood rise into my cheeks. Damn, couldn't I lie without blushing anymore? And it was only part of a lie or even less because in the beginning I hadn't taken the game seriously. Only later had I really started to care. I sat on my bare feet to keep the sight of them from embarrassing both of us.

"I would have failed miserably without you," went on Mr. Lauritzen. I wished he would stop. I had to stretch because my legs felt cramped. "I never could have kept my promise to Mrs. Lauritzen." He paused. "What are your plans now?"

There was mother and father's plan for me to go to boarding school; there was my plan to stay on my own and search for Jochen. I had long scrapped the former—in fact, from the very moment they had waved from the window and did not bother to come to the front door to say good-by. And now I realized that my later plan had changed too. I was not going to give up my independence or my search for Jochen, but I was not going to give up the old man either. I was not going to leave him when he still needed my help. I had to build a shelter, straighten his papers out with the authorities, steal and barter for a stove, a bed, and other necessities, and find a doctor for his cough. Tomorrow I would post a message for Jochen at the station in Cologne with his address.

"Could I stay with you for a few nights?" I asked.

"There may not be a place to stay." He smiled. "But you are welcome to it."

It was as nice a funeral as the attendant had promised. He had the grave dug and the coffin placed inside; he had arranged a wreath of greens with a white bow and a bunch of yellow daffodils; he even had lined up a priest instead of music. In my bare feet I stood on a pile of earth and threw three handfuls of dirt on the coffin. Mr. Lauritzen wept a little, coughed a lot, and wept some more.

Then we left the cemetery together. We had a lot of work to do and my stomach grumbled.

T. DEGENS grew up in eastern Germany. She studied biology in Bonn, immigrated to the United States in 1956, and now lives in Falmouth, Massachusetts. At present, Ms. Degens is in Germany with her husband and three sons, studying psychology at the University of Hamburg in preparation for extensive work with retarded people. She loves hiking and camping and hopes to walk the Appalachian Trail from end to end one of these days.